"He's a devil, that Grue!"

The man in front of Johnson was not overly tall, he only seemed that way with his gangling shape; so gaunt, Johnson thought, he'd have had to stand twice to cast a shadow. In a chin-strapped hat and that holstered pistol tied to his leg, any knowledgeable man could have guessed what his trade was. Hooked nose, the mouth a tight clamped gash in the cadaverous face, skin stretched tight and shiny across the bones of his cheeks.

All of this Johnson saw in that first swift glance, likewise the pair so still behind him. "If you've any legitimate business here state it."

The man cleared his throat, appeared to check the rush of temper. Something unreadable was at the edges of his stare. "Name's Grue. We're huntin' a couple of fugitives—one of them's a gitana."

Johnson seemed to be searching his mind. "Gypsy girl with a Injun stopped here—must of been all of ten days ago. Got the idea they was headed for Tucson. Now you know, you kin be on your way."

Grue began to look ugly. "Wonder if you're brash as you sound."

"Put your paw near that shooter, an' you'll know for sure."

*Nelson Nye books
from Jove*

BANDIDO
TREASURE TRAIL FROM TUCSON
GRINGO
MAVERICK MARSHAL
THE TROUBLE AT PEÑA BLANCA
A BULLET FOR BILLY THE KID

THE LOST PADRE
NELSON NYE

JOVE BOOKS, NEW YORK

THE LOST PADRE

A Jove Book/published by arrangement with
the author

PRINTING HISTORY
Jove edition/May 1988

ISBN: 0-515-09551-6

Jove Books are published by The Berkley Publishing Group,
200 Madison Avenue, New York, New York 10016.
The name "JOVE" and the "J" logo
are trademarks belonging to Jove Publications, Inc.

ONE

Teluride Johnson had been all over, from Bagdad to Tonopah, Bullfrog, Ballarat, Goldfield—you name it. He was the kind of galoot most at home in forgotten places, and these he searched out in run-over boots, following the tail of old Nugget, his burro. A man of unusual freewheeling convictions, crusty as a salt flat, kind to cripples, old ladies and gophers; a loner by choice, described by himself as a single-blanket jackass prospector, content to while away his days far as he could get from the maddening throng.

Been a time in his youth when he'd worked for a living, punching other folks' cattle for thirty and found. Brown as a boot, his sun-faded glance generally scrinched from the glare, wrinkles deep-cut from the scalding winds, wiry and lean as a half-starved coyote, you could have taken him for sixty instead of the thirty he measured in years.

He was camped on a spring—the only water in miles with the nearest town a good three days' ride; reason enough to feel what he was seeing had to be a mirage. He'd been gone all morning, returned to stretch out for his customary forty winks in the welcome shade of the three towering cottonwoods that landmarked the spring, when a nudge from old Nugget brought his eyes snapping open.

What he saw, incredibly, was the muzzle of a pistol in point-blank focus held in the hand of a determined-looking girl in the sweat-stained, brush-clawed garb of a gypsy and, some ten feet away, a pair of travel-gaunted ponies being kept from the water by a head-banded Apache with a Winchester repeater.

Teluride Johnson scrubbed at his eyes with a rock-scarred fist.

If this wasn't a mirage he had to be dreaming. He gave himself a pinch by way of making sure. The only change he could discern was that the girl—she couldn't, he thought, have been more than seventeen—appeared more riled than she had been at first glance.

A real looker, she was. Honey-colored skin with olive shadows, eyes that were greener than a new growth of grass, red-haired, notional and obviously crammed with the same kind of passion whitening the knuckles that were wrapped round that pistol.

"I said," she cried fiercely, "what are you doing here?"

"Reckon you kin see. I been takin' a nap."

This seemed only to antagonize her further. "I mean, what are you doing here on private property?"

"Comes to that," said Teluride Johnson, "what the heck are you doin' on my claim?"

"Claim!"

He thought, by grab, she was going to shoot him out of hand. It was there, plain as paint, in the flare of green eyes, in the way she stiffened, in the fiercening grip she had on that shooter.

"This land's already claimed. It was bought by my uncle more than forty years ago—it's in the name of my family! You can't claim land that is already owned!"

"Yes, well . . . That's where you're plumb out of luck," Johnson said. "In Arizona law—an' believe me, I should know!—the mineral rights are separate, they've got nothing to do with who owns the land. Go to any county courthouse an' they'll tell you the same."

"I don't believe it!" She skewered him with a bitter glance. "I won't be trifled with," she cried, stamping her foot in a furious fashion. "If you don't get up and go I'll put a hole right through you!"

"After which," said Teluride Johnson, "you're like to find yourself with a rope round your neck, bein' hanged for murder."

Her brows went up with the bark of a laugh. "Who'll ever know?"

She had something there.

"Who are you anyhow?" he said, stalling for time. "An' who's this uncle you been oratin' about?"

"My name," she said with her chin thrust out, regal as though to the manner born, "is Amita Maria Pintado y Morales of the Hacienda Villalobos, held by my people for more than two hundred years; chartered by the King of Spain, it covers almost one-third of the state of Sonora!"

Johnson smiled. "A likely tale."

She looked minded to shoot him then and there. She cuffed the wind-ruffled hair back away from her cheek. "Tell him where we come from, Jaime."

"Villalobos," answered the Apache, waving the rifle in the direction of Mexico.

"You hear?" she cried, stabbing Johnson with another of those ferocious stares. "Now get off my land at once— *andale, pronto!*"

She damn well meant it, he was in no doubt about that. But it went sore against the grain for Teluride Johnson to be ordered around like a mozo by anyone, let alone by a chit of a girl in a bunch of dang rags. "If you are who you claim to be what's the idea of that gypsy—"

"I am disguised," she cried with another lift of the chin. "I have run away—do you understand?"

"Run away, have you?"

"Don't you dare laugh at me!"

"All tattered an' torn—I wouldn't think of it," declared Teluride Johnson, solemn as an owl. "Why don't you tell me about it? Mebbe I kin help."

There was a pride in this girl, an arrogance too that,

combined with the posture, that assumption of status, tended to substantiate those preposterous claims. "But you talk like the place was a prison . . ."

"Yes!" She eyed him suspiciously. "For me it was a prison."

Johnson passed a hand across his bristles again. "But how could this be? If you're heir to—"

"No girl could be heir in that country. My brother's the heir." With a visible reluctance, "He's too weak to take care of me," she said. "The persons in charge—"

"And who would that be? In such an establishment . . ." Johnson caught himself up, almost beginning to believe her.

"The guardian, of course. Rube Haddam, the lawyer— we're orphans, you see. I am not of legal age and Luis, my brother, is younger still. And there is Brodie Grue— Haddam's gringo friend of the snaky eyes; they flatter Luis into doing what they want."

"And what's that?"

The green eyes flashed with anger. "To steal our heritage, of course!" she said bitterly.

"I don't see— Couldn't you go to the authorities?"

"Hah!" she exclaimed. "In Mexico many things are possible, but a female has no rights. They would laugh at me. Like Haddam! In my country all females are *slaves!*" She cried harshly: "We have only two choices—to pleasure some man or get married and raise babies!"

Johnson pulled off his hat to scratch at his head, finding this indictment a bit hard to swallow. Could be true enough with *pelados* and *peones,* but the daughter of a hidalgo . . .

She was eyeing him fiercely. "You think I make this up. Let me tell you, in my country money is everything. If you have money there are hands to open doors. Unless she is rich or a very great heiress a girl is nothing. At Villalobos I was less than nothing!"

"Hell's fire!" Johnson exclaimed. "I can't believe—"

"I am a prisoner in my own home. I had not one friend in that place but this poor Indian horse handler. We are two of a kind to be moved here or there according to the whim of this so-fat *abogado!* You see, there is this lost mine—'' A hand flew to her mouth. She looked at him horrified.

"A mine, eh?" Johnson brightened.

"I should not have said that . . ." She eyed him nervously.

"Might's well tell the rest of it, now."

The pistol, which both of them appeared to have forgotten, was suddenly jerked into wicked focus. The green eyes, frightened, furious, flashed like emeralds. "You are not to regard that. The mine belonged to my uncle, Father Eusibio."

"A priest? With a mine?"

She was plainly overwhelmed by the suddenly recognized extent of her folly.

"Go on—tell me about it," Johnson urged, displaying his Sunday smile.

But how could she trust him? A gringo! Better to shoot him right now and be done with it. As though he could read every thought she laid hold of he looked like a cat about to pounce on a mouse. She was realizing now she could not pull the trigger.

He said, "Come on—what can you lose? I said I'd help you. Can't go at it blind."

She sighed. "My Uncle Eusibio, to keep what he'd found, had to give up the priesthood. It was a long time ago. The Indians killed him."

Johnson nodded. "Sure. Just like the Peraltas. They had mines up here, too. How come this lawyer and his gringo friend haven't made any effort to find this mine?"

"I think they were getting ready to. There was a map . . ."

"Good grief, girl, maps to lost mines are a dollar a dozen!"

"Before Eusibio went back that last time I believe from things my father has said he was a worried man. He drew a map and told my father to hide it well. It was behind a brick in the sala chimney. Though I had often hunted it after his death it is scarcely a month since I made the discovery; they'd been watching me and took it away from me.

"I told my brother. They laughed at him. 'Ridiculous,' they said. 'If you believe that you'll believe anything.' So what could I do?

"I'd found out where Haddam kept it. I was desperate. It was in an old book under a stack in his bedroom, but except when he was there he kept the door locked. One night two weeks ago . . ." She shuddered in remembrance. "It seemed my last chance. When the house was asleep I crept into his bedroom. I was shaking like a leaf. I had my hand right on it when the bedsprings skreaked. I was in such a terror, so frantic I tore it; but he was only turning over, not really awake. I did not realize I had torn it until next day when we—Jaime and myself—had crossed the border."

Johnson considered her. He had been here two weeks and had found no trace of color. "How much of that map have you got?" he asked finally.

"The part that shows the three cottonwoods and the spring."

"That follows"—he nodded—"or you wouldn't be here." The Apache, he thought, looked to be getting a little restless. But long as the fellow was in sight, and this close, Johnson reckoned he could take him. "That's not what I asked."

She licked her lips, seemed to make up her mind. "I have a little more than half . . . But I've agreed if we find the mine to share it with Jaime—he helped me get away. If they'd caught us they'd have shot him, but I needed a guide and he was glad to get away; besides he knows all the tricks of hiding a trail—"

"You don't think you've been followed?"

"I'm sure we have," she admitted, looking a little grim, "but I don't think they'll find us. Before he was captured Jaime once lived in this country." She said on a sharper note: "If this is your claim where are the boundary stakes?"

"Well . . ." Johnson said, "I ain't got around to puttin' 'em down yet."

TWO

She eyed him awhile through a disconcerting silence. "I guess," she said with a kind of odd relish, "you're what they call a soldier of fortune—a mercenary whose services are available to the highest bidder."

Returning her stare, not entirely sure that remark was uncalled for, he reminded her with a wave of his arm that took in their surroundings, "I'm still the feller you're going to have to deal with. Possession round here carries considerable weight and," he said, grinning, "I'm in possession."

"Yes"—she smiled,—"but only until I shoot you."

Teluride Johnson loosed a great belly laugh. "Let's quit playin' games an' git down to brass tacks. A Mexican standoff ain't much use in this deal." With casual assurance he asked, still grinning, "How much you offerin' to have me in your camp?"

He watched her mouth tighten. "Eusibio's mine, if I've not been misled, is fabulously rich—"

"Rich enough for three?"

"From what I have heard I would think so. You can

judge for yourself," she called over her shoulder as she moved to her horse. A number of notions passed through his mind as he watched her reach into a saddlebag. When she turned back the gun no longer dangled from her hand; all she had in it was a chunk of rock about as large as a turkey's egg which she tossed in his direction without further words.

Reaching out a fist he deftly corraled it, lips pursed in a whistle as he held the piece of quartz up to the light, the better to examine it. It gave out flashes as he turned it over and the sun was reflected from the stringers of gold which laced the inside of it. "This came from your uncle's mine?"

"Where else would I get it?"

"I dunno. Could be one of them samples out of the Lost Dutchman."

"The Peralta mines were well north of here. In the Superstitions, were they not?"

"Accordin' to the legends," he acknowledged, again lifting a fist to rasp along his jaw as, with sharpening glance, he rummaged her face. "High-grade rock," he said at last. "Be enough where this come from to put us all on Easy Street—"

"Providing we find it and my partner agrees to split it three ways."

This fetched Johnson's head up. "Partner! What partner?"

"Why, Jaime, of course. As I've already told you I promised him half."

Pulling his stare off her Johnson fastened it on the Apache who, unaccountably, appeared to be finding some humor in this present situation. He still had the rifle in the crook of an arm.

An unsettling quiet appeared to permeate the passing moments. Amita Maria Pintado y Morales trotted out her silken smile. "Shall we take a vote?"

"No vote," the Apache grunted.

Johnson shrugged. "All right, we got a standoff." And perhaps, he thought, it was just as well; for if there was one thing he valued above all others it was his cherished independence, and the way this thing had been shaping up he had come within an ace of getting himself encumbered, carried away by this girl's fascination.

He tossed back her sample and went and sat down on the handiest rock.

"Well," she said brightly, "would you consider becoming a partner for half of my half?" And while she had him entangled in that, "What do we call you?" she asked of a sudden.

Jerked out of his thinking, Johnson said with a parched smile, "I can't see that it makes no never-mind, being we're not going on with this deal. Case of here today an' gone tomorrer."

"*We*'re not going anywhere till I've had a look for that mine," said Miss Pintado, folding both arms across her curves, a look in her eyes that bordered on ugly.

"Me, either," said Johnson, throwing the Indian a challenging look.

Jaime grinned. "I better water these horses."

"That spring's out of bounds," Johnson said.

Caught in the middle, the girl said sharply, "I see no occasion for fireworks. We should be able with goodwill to resolve this situation amicably."

"Go right ahead," Johnson nodded. "I make it a practice to do unto others the same way I'm done by."

The girl ran a pink tongue across her lips. "I suggest we stop acting like bickering children. Regardless of who was here first you're in no position to deny us the hospitality of that spring."

Johnson got up and stretched. "Matter of opinion," he reminded her. "Right now I've got squatter's rights to this water."

"If I were to have a few words with the sheriff—"

"Hop at it." He grinned. "Like to be a long walk when them horses give out."

"Oh!" she cried, stamping her foot. "Must you be so hateful? I've offered to make you a partner and if we find the mine to give you—"

"Yeah. Heard you the first time."

"Well, how could I be any fairer than that?"

"I can't see nothin' fair about givin' a igorant Injun twice what you offer a man of experience, a feller with savvy who happens to be sittin' on the only source of water in a three-days' ride."

He saw her chew at her lip but kept the most of his attention on the man with the rifle, ready to burst into action at the first hint of trouble. He hadn't lived with the buggers but he had known enough Indians to subscribe to the notion the only good ones were dead ones.

He watched Jaime like a hawk. The Apache's regard held no more charity than could be found on a knife's edge, and the grass-green eyes of the self-proclaimed hidalgo's daughter looked from one to the other as though she'd like to shake both of them.

Johnson wasn't a man who found it easy to back down, but he could see no likelihood of profit if this string was played out the way it appeared to be headed. One or both of them could be killed or incapacitated. It was the possibility of a lingering death which finally made him pull in his horns.

It was with a feeling of revulsion bordering on disbelief that he heard himself say, "All right. Water your horses. I'll cook up some grub and then we'll draw up a contract givin' me a quarter interest in anything we find."

The girl pulled a breath deep into her, and if her smile seemed a mite grim round the edges it was, just the same, in the nature of a peace offering. "I'll water the horses while Jaime sets up my tent."

So an uneasy truce was tentatively established.

THREE

Johnson was aware from past experience that lacking a better relationship the present working agreement was no more stable than walking on quicksand—fragile as a spider's web. A partnership had to be built on trust and where was there any trust in this one? The Apache resented Johnson's inclusion. Johnson resented the disproportionate share set aside for the Indian. And the girl, in all conscience with best claim to the mine, stood to come out of this the biggest loser.

Like most things, if you could stomach them, the answer was simple. Eliminate one of the men and the survivors could draw equal shares from the mine.

He could see little use in this discovery. Until the mine was found there would be nothing here for anyone. He told himself for two cents he'd pull out—yet why the hell should he, being first on the ground?

But a feeling of injustice is a hard thing to live with, and the prospect of having to be continually on guard was anything but a salubrious one. There'd be risk in sleeping, risk every time your back was turned. He couldn't stay awake indefinitely and the first bit of carelessness was apt to be his last. What it all boiled down to, near as he could figure, was which got his knife in the other one first.

With her tent set up, and a rope encircling it to keep out the snakes, Amita Maria Pintado y Morales retired for the night soon after they'd wolfed down Johnson's grub.

After cleaning their supper tools by scrubbing them with sand, Johnson made ready to follow suit. He fed old Nugget and turned him loose, picked up his blanket and went back and sat down with his back to a boulder twenty feet beyond the spring, half-expecting the Apache to try and outsit him.

Jaime, however, paid him no attention. After caring for his horses and anchoring them to stakeropes he went off into the blackest shadows and was seen no more before daylight.

Johnson spent an exasperating night, cramped by his reluctance to provide any sound which might tend to make him a target. Further strain came from listening into the intense quiet that surrounded the campsite after the cicadas and crickets had signed off, trying without avail to pick up the slither of moccasined feet.

He was not, accordingly, at his most sociable when, having built up his fire with dried twigs and moldy cow turds, he set about preparing a breakfast of wheatcakes and sowbelly gingerly flavored with a few drops of sorghum from his dwindling store.

First to appear after he dropped the coffee beans into the pot of boiling water was the girl's Apache partner, black hair held in place by a red cloth headband. "Help youself," Johnson said, motioning toward the big stack of wheatcakes. Jaime ignored him but dumped the whole stack into one of the pans and stepped past the fire to stand wolfing them down. He was a hard man to like.

Johnson managed to keep hold of his temper, but only just barely. When the girl presently came from her tent with a cheerful greeting Johnson had another stack of griddlecakes ready but the sod-pawing mood heated up by the red man's studied insolence could still be detected in the cloudy eyes and deepened lines of his face. A surly grunt was the most she could get out of him and the crackling silence round the breakfast fire was so crammed with storm signals she was practically on tiptoes when she passed him her plate. Johnson dropped his eggshells into the bubbling coffeepot, filled her plate, filled a tin mug from the battered pot and strode off to give Nugget a measure of oats.

When he returned some minutes later she was still by the fire taking cautious sips of the tantalizing brew. "This is very good," she said hopefully, but all this elicited from the cook was a sound like the growl of an angry dog.

Miss Pintado managed to take this in stride and as Johnson started packing up the sand-scrubbed pots and pans she said in a surprisingly businesslike manner, "Before we start searching I think you had better have a look at this," and handed him a much creased and rather grubby-looking bit of paper. "Uncle Eusibio's map," she explained.

Her look was so appealing that, somewhat mollified, he found himself accepting the offering and smoothing it out, though the look of his face was no less bleak. Grimly studying the drawing—and it took a deal of study to separate the faded lines from the wrinkles—he heard her say, "You'll notice the spring with the trees in the upper left-hand corner. I imagine this must be the starting point. Unfortunately, as you can see, the part with the 'X' representing the mine must have been on the piece that tore off."

Johnson scowled. "I expect you're right. What we've got suggests the mine's location has to be off someplace southeast of here. All the prospecting I've done has been north an' west of the spring. And I kin tell you for sure there's nothing up there. Let's see," he muttered, going over it again. "What we need to get properly started is a compass . . ."

The girl nodded. "I've got one. You brought up the possibility yesterday," she said, "of Haddam and Brodie Grue tracking us here. I don't believe they can do it. If you could have seen Jaime's efforts to confuse our tracks at every possible point . . . He certainly understood that if those devils caught up with us the first thing they'd do would be to shoot him dead."

Johnson nodded, still eyeing the map.

Biggest barrier to such an accomplishment, even recalling the spring with three trees, was that this, presumably, was the starting point. Lacking this in relation to other features stressed in the drawing, even if they should recollect and locate one of these, they were unlikely to remember which way to go from it to the next.

The fact that the "X" was on the scrap they held could hardly be of much use to them unless it could be correlated to the references he had under his hand. He'd attempted to track treasure from maps before and was pretty well convinced they'd get no place without the entire map. Unless they knew the country thoroughly and had been over it in person he reckoned he could forget them. There were no shortcuts in the treasure-hunting business.

He'd read everything he could find on this subject and the times people had stumbled onto the jackpot could be counted on one hand with fingers left over.

"Seems that from here we head south for about six miles to a sandstone butte in a sunken area whose top can't be seen from the surrounding country. So our first job of work is to find that butte."

He looked up to find Miss Pintado watching him intently. "What," she asked, "do we do about water?"

"We take all we can carry and hope it will be enough. I've got two canvas waterbags and each of you have got one. Fill them now and make them last. If we run out of water we'll be in a real bind."

He gave her back the map and made ready to move. He called Nugget, fastened the packsaddle on him, secured his filled waterbags, lashed aboard his dwindling supplies and cooking and eating utensils, drew his Sharps from its sheath and looked around for his companions.

The Apache gave the girl a leg up, swung onto his own horse and chucked a curt nod in Johnson's direction. Johnson led off with rifle in hand, the girl came next with Jaime bringing up the rear, an arrangement Johnson didn't like a little bit. "Didn't you mention," he said to the girl, "this Injun had been in these parts before?" When she nodded, he said, "Then he'd better take the lead," and motioned the Apache ahead of them.

With the girl behind the Indian and his burro behind the girl, Teluride Johnson walked behind Nugget after returning the Sharps buffalo gun to its sheath on the packsaddle. With compass in hand to correct any notions Jaime might be coddling and his Colt's six-shooter swinging at his hip, Johnson found time to cull some notions of his own.

There was, he admitted, a slim possibility the Apache *might* be loyal to the girl, but there was no doubt in his mind that so far as Johnson was concerned Jaime was distinctly hostile. Waiting only for a chance to be rid of him.

It was crowding noon of a very warm morning when they came to a drop-off ledge and saw the butte they'd been hunting directly ahead in the narrow canyonlike valley spread below them. The valley itself was perhaps a mile-and-a-half long and Johnson was looking for a way to get down when Miss Pintado, consulting her map, spoke up to say, "From the butte we're supposed to go east five miles—due east—to reach a 'sugarloaf hill' turned broadside to the course of our travel. Here—you look," she urged, handing him the map.

"That's right," he said, examining it. "Five miles due east from the butte. We'll rest here for a bit to give the animals a breather."

The Apache, following Johnson's example, poured a small amount of water into a couple of nosebags and gave both horses a drink. Neither he nor Johnson took any themselves and the girl, seeing this, followed suit, thus winning a nod of approval from Teluride Johnson, who was considerably chagrined when it occurred to him as it several times did how easily he'd been led into sticking his neck out by joining this venture. Being cumbered with a female of any stripe had never been a part of his plans. Eyeing her covertly he was forced to the conclusion that for a female—and a dude besides—she was acquitting herself surprisingly well.

For a while now their way led across reasonably level

ground, a sandy waste whose only adornment was cholla, pear and an occasional yucca with waxy bell-like flowers standing out from its staff. Ahead, off in the heat-blurred distance, he could see the blue shapes of a line of low hills.

At the end of an hour, seeing her flushed face, he insisted on her taking a couple mouthfuls of water. Since their pace had to be accommodated to the measure of his strides it was nearing five o'clock when at last they spotted the sugarloaf hill marked on the map as the second stage of their journey. With the animals stopped he asked what was next as though he couldn't remember.

"From this hill," she said, "we go south again for two miles to 'a great heap of rocks' and, from there, due southeast to a 'lone saguaro in a forest of silver-spined cholla.' "

"Reckon," Johnson said, "we better camp right here an' make an early start in the cool of the morning." And the girl, anyway, was glad to get down.

After feeding and watering Nugget from his hat Johnson made a small fire of greasewood sticks, lifted the supplies and packsaddle off his burro and watched a moment while Nugget rolled to get the cramps from his back, bounded erect and vigorously shook himself, blowing through his nose with evident satisfaction. Meanwhile the Apache was putting up the girl's tent, not forgetting the hair rope to ward off snakes.

FOUR

It had been said of Johnson he was built like a snake on stilts, which likely came from so many years of fixing his own food; but on this occasion with Miss Pintado seeming a mite tuckered and all he dug into his supplies with a reckless hand to provide a supper of throat-tickling grub. He served pooch, whistle-berries, gun-wadding bread and for dessert a special treat of boggy-top pie, a bit on the skimpy side being made out of air-tights saved from two days ago, but pie nonetheless.

He was unable to guess how these delicacies struck her but reckoned they must have slid down pretty easy because nothing was left on her tin when they'd finished. While he was scouring up their eating tools with sand she walked over to say, "I don't suppose you've ever cooked on a ranch . . ."

"Well, no—not to say cooked; I put in some months on the Hashknife though before Burt Mossman tore the outfit apart."

"Have you ever shot a man?—killed him, I mean?"

He stared with his brows up. "Round these parts it

ain't considered polite to pry into a man's past with them kind of questions. But to give a straight answer I'd have to say yes—not that they hadn't been a long time needin' it.''

She gave a brief nod as though in confirmation of whatever it was she'd been rolling around behind the screen of her eyes. ''Then if Haddam and that bare-faced gringo did happen to come onto us I could rely on you . . . ? I ask because right away, of course, they'd take care of Jaime.''

Johnson blinked. ''Thought you said there wasn't no chance of them catchin' up with us?''

''I don't believe there is, but you have to remember they are very resourceful.''

He said offhand, ''Any time I can't handle a couple of dudes—''

''Perhaps I've given you the wrong impression. Haddam, my guardian for several months yet, is a city man, of course, but this gringo only *wears* city clothes. He's . . . everyone knows he's a *pistolero.*''

Johnson's throat got a little dry. ''You mean he's a gunfighter?''

When she nodded he said brashly, ''Well, don't let it bother you. Chances are you've seen the last of them.''

''I would like to think so,'' she said with a sigh that seemed so forlorn he was moved to comfort her and only just managed to hobble his lip. Shaking his head like he'd run into a cobweb he peered around for the Indian. ''He's gone off,'' she said, ''to play tricks with our tracks.''

Johnson's thoughts were still hooked on the snag of that gunfighter. ''Who *is* this Brodie Grue pelican?''

She didn't actually shudder but some sort of revulsion ran noticeably through her. ''He's the one that lawyer is forever at me to marry. I'd sooner die!'' she said fiercely. ''You've no idea the things he gets up to . . . I'm scared to be alone in the same room with him.''

Johnson found his jaws clenched in sympathy and was ready right then to lay down his life for her, but while her green eyes were staring out over the range in one of those faraway looks that seemed sometimes to come over her he found the chance to recall that females—no matter how comely—had no place at all in his plans and told himself he had better wake up.

Then she said apropos of nothing he could catch hold of, "Mother was the only *gitana* who ever married into the Pintado family."

He exclaimed, astonished, "You—you mean your mother was a gypsy?" It didn't seem possible.

"Oh, yes . . . A famous flamenco dancer. These were some of her things I put on to escape in."

Chewing on that awhile Johnson asked, "How long have your folks been . . ."

"Dead, you mean? It is nearly a year since Papa was gored by a bull in the plaza at Cuenca—"

"Mean to say"—Johnson stared with dropped jaw—"your father was a *bullfighter?*"

Her brows jumped as though in his abysmal ignorance this gringo was incredible. "Of course not!" She appeared to be struggling to put the whole matter in words even a child should be able to understand but she couldn't connect them and said very loftily: "My father was a *gentleman,* one of the wealthiest men in the state of Sonora— a *hacendado!* The bull escaped and crashed through the barrier; that is how my papa was killed."

"And your mother?"

"No, she was not with him that day. She was killed in a fall from the tower window, only a few weeks ago. A terrible accident, they said, but I wouldn't believe it—she was too much alive to fall out of anything. In a closed coffin they buried her and wanted me to sign a great sheaf of papers . . . And when I would not listen to Haddam they locked me into my room until, they said, I should come to my senses."

"And then the Indian helped you escape?"

"Later. Not then. After I said I would not marry *anyone* Brodie Grue came one night to my room. He had taken off his spurs but I heard the tap of his heels on the corridor tiles and the sound of the key turning back the

lock and I was behind the door when it opened. It was
very dark in there, you understand, for they would not
allow me even so much as a candle at night, but I could
see him in the light from the corridor. And when he crept
toward the bed I struck him across the head with the heel
of my slipper, and when he fell down I struck him
again.''

Johnson's mouth was tight with a mean-looking temper.
''That's when you ran away?''

''Yes. I stole out to the stables and Jaime said he would
get me away from there. I wanted to get the other piece
of the map, but he wouldn't wait . . .'' She said after a
moment, ''He tried to get my father's horse—this was the
one the lawyer used and they had El Capitano locked
away in a place by himself and Jaime was afraid it would
make too much noise to get at him. So we took two
horses from the day corral, and that was how we left
Villalobos.''

It was too much, he thought, for a man to swallow, yet
a ring of truth had leapt from her voice which he found
was hard to set aside. The story she told plagued him most
of the night and when he got up to put on hat and boots
it was not yet light but he was pushed by the threat of that
gringo gunfighter. The fellow would be frothing to get
hold of her now, would cling to their trail like a leech,
Johnson reckoned. Haddam might settle for maneuvering
the heir but Grue's vanity had suffered; what the girl had
done must have cost him much face and his kind of var-
mint couldn't stand to be laughed at.

No, he'd be on their trail and all Jaime's tricks would
only delay him a little. So time was important, and time
was passing.

He whistled up Nugget, fed him some oats and gave
him a drink and threw the packsaddle on in a flutter of
impatience. When he saw Jaime watching he said, ''Wake
the girl. We're gettin' out of here.''

When she came from the tent the Apache dismantled
it while Johnson questioned her about the next stage of
their journey. ''We turn directly south again for two

exact miles—that's what the map says. Then west six miles to the side of a bald mountain that's a jumble of boulders.''

"All right," Johnson said. "We'll eat when we get there."

FIVE

But when they got to the mountain Johnson felt like he'd been fried without grease and, but the glare of that sun in a cloudless sky, it couldn't get anything but hotter. There was nothing in front of them but a vast pile of rocks, boulders big and little with several great rocks like broken cliffs thrusting out of them, dun colored, stark and dappled with shadows, like something spewed up by some gigantic upheaval in the time of the dinosaurs. Not a blade of grass nor a tree could be seen. "Looks near enough to hell to smell the smoke," Johnson said with a grimace.

After that not a sound broke the monstrous quiet until the Apache, dismounting, dug from his saddlebags several flour tortillas that looked like gray napkins and a four-ounce tin of refried beans which he sliced open with a bowie knife and passed around. "Just put the beans in your tortilla," the girl advised Johnson. "That's how we make bean burros."

They tasted better than they looked. After he'd consumed a little more than half with Nugget at his elbow watching every bite with eager eyes and a curled-back lip,

Johnson held the rest of it out to the burro, who took it daintily with evident relish.

"We cross these rocks by an old smuggler's trail," Miss Pintado announced. "I don't see any trail but—"

"There is trail," the Apache said. "We hunt snakes in there when I was boy."

Johnson gave him a long hard look. "What else do you know about this mountain?"

The Indian shrugged. "Great place for accident."

"Yeah," Johnson said, and was pretty near sure he'd seen amusement back of that enigmatic dark brown stare. "Make damn sure you're not involved." After giving that time to sink in, he said, "Mebbe we should wait a bit. Right now them rocks'll be hotter'n the devil's backlog."

The Indian's pleasure was plain when he said, "Snakes crawl at night."

"An' some snakes walk on two legs," Johnson growled.

"I think," the girl said, looking from one to the other, "we had better push on."

"Just a minute." Johnson pushed out a hand. "If we're goin' on with this . . ."—he gave the redman a mighty plain look—"we better have some straight talk. There's two of us here got maggoty minds and unless we kin bury the hatchet right now there's damn little use goin' one step farther."

The Indian grunted. "What white chief say make good horse sense," and held out a hand with the palm side up.

Johnson looked a long while before he finally took it, giving the Apache a grudging grin. "Until we find the mine," he couldn't help saying. Then, "As chief shareholder in this enterprise what do you figure we ought to do now?"

"I had a look at that map before it got torn," Jaime said, no longer bothering to act the dumb Injun, "and there was no 'X' anyplace on it. It's my belief that priest fixed up this map for his brother—Amita's father—and halfway through got a change of mind. Near as I can recall there's nothing beyond this part of the map that could possibly grow any gold-bearing ore."

Johnson pushed that around. "You mean the mine's buried someplace in this part of the map?"

"If there *is* a mine it's got to be. Like you said a while back, that sample Amita's got could have come from the Dutchman. But assuming Eusibio really did have a mine I'll give odds it's on this part of the map. As I understand it, when gold in commercial quantity is found on a flat some time in the past there was a mountain over it. Why look elsewhere? We've got a mountain right here."

Against his druthers Johnson felt the man was right. With a grimace he tipped his head in a nod. "Bitch of a place to have to hunt fer it," he growled, eyeing askance that monstrous pile of boulders with the heat waves curling over them, baked for how many centuries and, still baking, in the sun.

He felt dry and brittle, almost like an old man, as he stood beside Nugget, contemplating the prospect. "Be worse'n huntin' the proverbial needle!" He let out a great sigh. "If there's a trail goin' through there we better start lookin' for it."

Jaime found where the smuggler's trail had been ground into the slope's detritus, and rock dust rose in an enveloping cloud as they went staggering and lurching on a climbing tangent through that boulder-packed maze. "God pity the snakes that have to live here!" Johnson muttered through a dust-clogged throat.

After a full half hour of hellish travel, standing soaked in sweat and dust turned to mud on every bit of exposed skin, looking back he reckoned they hadn't gained more than a quarter of a mile. "Once we get beyond that three-hundred-foot cliff," Jaime gasped, "the trail opens out into a kind of glen. A pretty good place to camp. Been used quite a lot over the years I'd say."

Nobody else said anything. When they got back enough breath to go farther into this purgatory (as Johnson thought of it) he sighted a buzzard circling high above and lugubriously reckoned the bird wouldn't have no great while to wait for the chance to pick over some good fresh meat.

During the next hour of their horrible heat-drenched

progress he counted six more scavengers that had joined the first cooly sailing the air currents high above as they continued to keep tabs on the prospective feast.

Now, at last, the smugglers' trail was beginning to swing, with sudden drops to be skirted with care, around the base of the tan clifflike butte. A quarter hour later the glen mentioned by Jaime abruptly opened out before them showing the gray scars of old campfires, a couple of hackberries, four young cottonwoods attempting to push through the shade of a large rough-barked old one reaching almost to the top of the butte on this side. And, like paradise glimpsed, a bright pool of clear water obviously fed by hidden springs.

Johnson, staring like he couldn't believe it, watched old Nugget trot to the edge and thrust his muzzle deep into it. The two horses, apparently eager to join him, were being held back by Jaime's hands on their bridles. The burro, perhaps not really smarter than his large cousins but with that keen sixth sense which abounds in his kind, pulled his head up and blew through his nostrils before bending once more to daintily lip at the water.

The girl, dismounting, sank exhausted onto the grass. "You knew about this?" said Johnson hoarsely to the Apache.

Jaime nodded. "Reckoned it would do you more good if it came as a surprise. Been twenty years since I was here; wasn't sure those springs were still working."

Johnson dug out a cup and half filled it for the girl. "Take your time—don't gulp it down," he advised, and cuffed Nugget with affection as the burro came over to be unloaded. Jaime now led the pair of horses to the pool, not letting them drink near as much as they wanted, pulling them away and knotting the reins to one of the cottonwoods while he stripped them of gear and lifted off the saddles. Then he set up the tent in the shadow of the hackberries. "This ought to make us a first-rate base. Exploring this mountain's going to take some time."

Johnson got himself a small drink and began making preparations for supper. It wasn't yet time for putting on the nosebags but if the rest felt the way he did a good hearty meal couldn't come too soon. His supplies were considerably lower than he liked but he still had a good ten pounds of dried pintos and, with water at hand, he put a batch on to boil.

The girl had retired to her tent with a bucket of water after he'd allowed her another drink. Jaime refilled their waterbags and gathered up an armful of sticks for the fire and when the girl presently reappeared Johnson had to look twice to realize it was her in the suede riding skirt and linen blouse the color of blue larkspur, sorrel hair pulled back and held in place by a highbacked Spanish comb.

He never said a word though it was plain he was impressed. Jaime smiled. "How nice you look," and Johnson saw the touch of color in her cheeks.

She said to him, "Do you think we can find it?"

"We'll sure give it a good try."

When the beans were about done he pushed the kettle back a bit where the heat from the stones would keep them simmering and put the pot Jaime had filled over the flames and when it started bubbling dropped in a handful of coffee beans. Then he whipped up some biscuits and when all was ready they sat down to eat.

"Don't forget that hair rope," Johnson said when they had finished.

"Too bad we haven't a dog," Jaime said, looking round. Dusk was already falling across the lower slopes. The buzzards had disappeared. Quite a number of smaller birds were nesting in the cottonwoods and two hawkmoths were swooping above the pool when the girl, calling good night, went into her tent. "Don't reckon we'll need to put out a guard," Johnson said. "Not yet, anyway."

The Indian said, "I don't imagine they'll find us here, but they'll be hunting us, you can depend on that. Haddam's greed won't leave him alone and Brodie Grue will be nursing a big hate. He figured to marry into that family and get a bigger chunk of the spoils Haddam's been salting away. If I was in Haddam's shoes I think I'd be worrying a heap about him."

"What sort of jigger is this gunfightin' Grue?"

"*Muy peligroso*—dangerous and mean. What's worse, he's got no more sense than a two-year-old kid. I remember a cat he hung up by the tail. You never heard such a racket. Sat himself down just out of reach, grinning and chuckling while he watched it screech and squirm. And a dog whose front feet he chopped off with a cleaver."

SIX

In all the vast state of Sonora there was nothing that even approached in size and grandeur the Hacienda Villalobos. There were other haciendas, some of these quite notable, yet in no sense to be compared. Villalobos was the epitome, covering the most land, employing the most *peones*, producing the most wealth and by far the best managed.

To all intents and purposes it was a self-sufficient kingdom, for its army of retainers truly a way of life. Its whitewashed walls, red tiles, towers and imposing gates were pictured on thousands of tourist postcards, more familiar than the governor's face. It produced the finest horses, hundreds of tons of maize and alfalfa, cattle in the thousands. Over the years the family had given the country four generals, an admiral, legislators beyond count, three bishops and a cardinal. Also a pair of governors.

On the morning following Amita's departure everything seemed in unprecedented confusion, people scurrying hither and yon, schedules disrupted, traditions trampled, shouts and yells the order of the day. If Villalobos wasn't turned upside down it was certainly shaken to its very foundations. Calls and orders and the pounding of hoofs seemed everywhere as the establishment was searched from one end to the other. Prayers and frightened faces abounded. By the end of the day it was fearfully acknowledged that Amita Maria Pintado y Morales had unaccountably vanished.

In the great sala of the house Brodie Grue in jangling spurs and dust-powdered clothing paced the tiles in savage outrage while the fat triple-chinned Haddam, family lawyer and legal guardian of the missing girl, cowered in his chair, a veritable ghost of his customary importance, shaken like a jelly each time Grue wheeled a look at him.

"Don't tell me! That little bitch has run away!" Grue shouted, "How long was I out?"

"How can I tell?" Haddam quavered. "She was not in her room when the *mosa* looked in with her chocolate. Only one other cannot be found—that Apache, Jaime, who worked with the horses."

"She's run off with that Indian . . . I'll castrate the bastard! Do you hear? And when we catch up with them I'll fix her good! Find me some of the Indian's clothes. I'll take that horse you've been gallivantin' round on and that feller you fetched in here as foreman—what's his name?"

"Brusco Melindroso."

"Yeah, and that Yaqui tracker! Get yourself ready. We depart in an hour."

"Me?" The lawyer was horrified. "Impossible! You know I dare not leave the heir—and I've yet to get the accounts in order. Anyway, you cannot leave before morning . . . Who can search out tracks in the dark?"

"Another thing!" Grue pinned him with a fiery look. "I'll want them bloodhounds! *Andale, pronto!*"

"But how can you tell which way they went?"

"She's off to hunt for that mine, of course! They'll go north past Nogales and Peña Blanca—I'll find them!" He glared at the fat man. "There's a mark on the shoe of one of those horses—I'll find them, all right!"

Teluride Johnson, after Jaime's disclosures, was a long time getting to sleep that night. He had no doubt at all that sooner or later that *pistolero,* Grue, was going to catch up with them. It might be a week, two weeks maybe, but sure as God made little green apples that sonofabitch was going to be round here. And when he came there was like to be hell to pay.

He could think of no way to guard against it short of taking himself straight out of this jackpot. And for all his gruff ways he couldn't do that. Mine or no mine, he wasn't the kind to leave that girl in this fix. It graveled him plenty to come up with this notion, to realize Amita had some way managed to get her hooks into him—him who all his whole life had fought shy of entanglements, prizing his vaunted independence above all things.

He cursed in a passion.

When he finally dozed off he got little rest for the wildness of his dreams and got up in the morning red-eyed and irascible, feeling as though he'd been pulled through a knothole.

Birds were singing in the cottonwoods. Jaime was nursing a tiny fire of dead sticks, smokeless after the Apache way, and the sun was just coming over the rimrocks. "Where the hell do we start lookin'?" he growled at the Indian.

Jaime shrugged and put on the coffee. "Reckon you should know more about that than me. Didn't you claim to be a prospector?"

Johnson swore. He peered around disparagingly. "Could be anyplace," he grumbled. "Just look at them goddam rocks!"

"Few things in this life come easy." Jaime grinned. "Guess we'll just have to keep looking till we find it."

"A rousin' prospect!"

"One thing we can look for is charred wood, rusted cans, things like that. Most of the palefaces I've been around have been pretty careless. Anything they can't use gets chucked out of their way—old papers, broken things. We could look for old fires."

"Easier to find an old dump," Johnson mentioned. "You can't mine ore without leavin' a dump." He poured himself some coffee, still looking around. "You never seen nothin' like that when you was round here as a kid?"

"Near the top of the mountain there's a dump," Jaime said. "Big hole, too. We didn't see any gold. Just a lot of big snakes, hissing and scrambling around all over. Nobody wanted to go down that hole."

"What makes 'Mita think Indians killed her uncle?"

"All I know is he never came back." He looked past Johnson in the tent's direction. "Here she comes now. Why not ask her?"

Johnson did. The girl said, "When he left on that last trip, according to Papa, he had three men with him. Only one returned to tell the story. He said Indians had killed everyone but him."

"And where is he now?"

"He was killed in an accident right after Grue arrived at Villalobos."

Johnson nodded. "Another accident. How many does that make since Grue showed up?"

The green eyes widened. Johnson said, "Let's see. There was your father, gored by a bull. Your mother falls out of a tower window. This man from the mine. Who else?"

The girl was watching him, shocked and wondering. Jaime said, "There was the old majordomo, forty years at Villalobos. The lawyer two days later hired a new foreman, a man named Melindroso. Some friend, they say, he had gone to school with. Him and Grue had their heads together plenty."

"And this Haddam, the lawyer . . . Another of Grue's friends?"

The Indian said, "At first, maybe. I think he was afraid of Grue."

"Case of thieves fallin' out?"

"Probably."

"Did this Haddam always live at Villalobos?"

"He always handled a great deal of our affairs, the legal things," Amita said. "He came after Papa was gored by the bull."

"And has lived there ever since," Jaime said.

The girl nodded. "He keeps the books, the accounts."

"Prob'ly shuffles things round to suit himself," Johnson growled. "Great opportunity for a man with few scruples. When we find this mine and you go home again better bring in an accountant to go over those books."

After breakfast the two men set out on foot to do some exploring and see what they could find. It was slow work and increasingly arduous as the sun climbed higher and the rocks heated up. "There's got to be some sign of a cleared space where they made camp," Johnson remarked. But the Indian looked dubious.

"If they were killed in a raid by Apaches forty years ago I doubt if there'll be much to go on now. If Indians killed them they'd hide the mine, change enough of the landscape to make sure no one else happened onto it."

"How about lower down?"

"We played all over those lower slopes. Maybe we've bit off more than we can chew. This mountain is about ten miles long by maybe five wide. Take us a year to cover it thoroughly."

"So we'll do the best we can," Johnson grunted. "Can you recollect any other glens like this? Any places at all that were free of rocks?"

"Several, but none with water. We stayed within a mile of this trail. Even Indians can sometimes get lost," Jaime said.

They'd brought a little water, a Winchester and the Sharps and a few strips of jerky to keep their stomachs quiet. During the course of the morning they came onto three small spaces that might possibly have been campsites but only one yielded any charred wood and this looked too fresh to have been there forty years.

They kept on hunting and were just about to start back to the glen where they'd left Amita when they came onto a scatter of human bones, bleached and brittle. Jaime reached down and showed Johnson a belt buckle, tarnished and bent pretty much out of shape. They had both seen buckles like it, handcrafted by Mexicans. The design was an old one, long discontinued.

Johnson, regarding the bones, said, "Could have been one of Eusibio's men. Let's do some more looking."

Ten minutes later Jaime found the skull with the top beaten in. Johnson, rearranging the bones, thought the fellow might have been around five feet ten. "Take another look around," he said. "See if any of these rocks look like they'd been moved."

They could not find any evidence of that, and no other relics were discovered. But there seemed to be what might once have been a trail zigzagging its way toward one of the peaks. "You ever been up there?" Johnson asked. The Indian shook his head. "Only peak we got onto was that flat-topped one." He pointed it out. "The one with the hole and the snakes."

"We'll take a look at it tomorrow." Teluride Johnson scrubbed at his jaw. "Seems pretty obvious from what you've said, but sometimes the obvious things are the right ones."

SEVEN

Amita seemed powerfully glad to see them to judge by the way her face lighted up. "You were gone so long I didn't know what to think. Tomorrow," she declared, "I'm going with you!"

They could see she'd been worried and gave her no argument. Johnson said, "We'll take Nugget, too. Then, if you give out we'll put you up on him. Surefooted as a mountain goat. He likes you, too. Must be all them tidbits you give him."

She said, flushing, "I didn't think you'd noticed. It's all right, isn't it?"

"Sure. He'll eat just about anything. Last year he chewed up one of my boots—most of it anyhow. See you've gathered up a big pile of sticks. Guess I better git to work on supper."

He opened up a good-sized can of corned beef, one of tomatoes and one of tinned corn, once he'd got the fire to his liking. The girl had already boiled up some java. After the canned stuff had been hotted up he whipped up some dough which he dribbled into tiny piles in a heated skillet and made cornmeal biscuits.

Sometimes, Johnson thought, Jaime could be and talk the compleat stupid Injun. But sometime or other he must have had some fairly comprehensive schooling for, when so inclined, he could speak as well as anyone, even occasionally using eighty-five-cent words and a few Johnson hadn't heard of. Sometimes studying him while talking this way you knew, looking into his expressive face, the fellow was at least as smart as most of the whites in this part of the country. It had in fact begun to come over Johnson that Indians maybe weren't much different than the rest of the human two-legged specimens.

After most of the grub he'd fixed had been eaten and they were all in a mellower frame of mind Johnson asked where Jaime and his relations had lived in this country.

"We had a camp at the foot of this mountain," Jaime answered.

"How'd you happen to turn up at Villalobos?"

"Ten, maybe twelve years ago, I was with a hunting party a long way south of here. We ran into this bunch of Mexicans; turns out they were traders. During the pow-wow we got into a squabble. There was a heap of killing and, next thing I remember, I was folded over a pony, tied hand and foot. It was that way I arrived at Villalobos. They watched me pretty close for a while. After they figured I was settled in they made me a *caverango*—a horse handler."

"Didn't they reckon you'd try to escape?"

"Guess they figured I never had it so good." Jaime grinned. "My turn now. How'd you come to be a prospector?"

"That's a long story. To cut it down to handlin' size, as the feller said, I reckon you'd call me a hunter. I was always one for the lonesome places, liked to poke around off by myself. I got caught up in lost mines—"

"Did you find any?" Amita asked, plainly interested.

"I found a couple. Didn't amount to much." Thinking

she seemed a mite disappointed, he said, "Kept me in grub fer a couple of years."

"Do you think Uncle's mine will be like that?"

Johnson shrugged. "Hard to tell. High-grade sometimes comes in pockets."

They sat around awhile longer, mostly talking to hear their heads rattle, then the Apache went off to tend his horses and Amita, keeping her voice down, said confidentially, "I think you should know he's given me back half his share in the mine."

Running this through his notions Johnson presently said with only a tinge of reluctance, "Reckon he's a pretty good sort. For an Injun."

After he'd given Nugget the few leftovers from supper he shook out his blanket and scuffed him a place for his hips under the cottonwoods.

Didn't take him so long to get to sleep as he'd reckoned. He kept thinking about Jaime, unable to decide if he could be taken at face value or was playing some dark game of his own, just biding his time to fling the hatchet. He hadn't got this close to any Indians before.

Must have been along about the middle of the night when he was suddenly jerked upright by a scream from the tent. Flinging aside his blanket, Johnson lunged to his feet, had six-shooter in hand and was crouched for a charge when the Apache's voice called out of the dark, "Horses been in a sweat. All right now. Just a mountain lion having a nightmare. Go back to sleep. Ain't nothing goin' to get you."

Next morning as they sat around the fire eating the "saddle blankets" he'd fried in his skillet, Amita asked Johnson, "Did you hear that mountain lion last night?"

"Can't say as I did, but no need to worry. They have to be bad hurt or almighty hungry to go after a person—a kid maybe, not grown-up people."

Amita shivered in remembrance. "I thought it was right outside the tent." Hesitating, she said nervously, "Do you think we're apt to run into one?"

"Don't seem too likely. Same way with snakes. Leave 'em alone they'll go about their business." He looked around. "Reckon we better get whackin'."

Having thought about it some, Johnson started her out on the back of Nugget as they worked their way between boulders to the place he and Jaime had quit at yesterday. Of course, right away she spotted the bones. "Prob'ly one of your uncle's men," Johnson mentioned. "Likely heatin' his axles when a tomahawk got him. Jaime found a belt buckle. You kin get down now, be easier walkin' here for a bit."

Jaime said, "I'll go first, kind of scout out the path," and took off, Amita following, the burro next and Johnson bringing up the drag. It was about halfway to noon, the sun heating up with its customary skill. With the sweat commencing to drip off their noses they came onto the first wide place they had seen since leaving the bones. There were bones here, too, the bleached-dry relics of a man who'd died in flight. This one had an arrow between his ribs.

The girl shivered. "Do you suppose your people did this, Jaime?"

The Apache picked up the arrow, took a good look at it. "Could be," he grunted. "Apache arrow, all right."

"Where are they now?"

Jaime showed a grim smile. "I'll give odds they're not here."

"Do you suppose they're the ones who hid the mine?"

"We don't know that it's hidden."

"That's right," Johnson said. "We don't know a damn thing." He peered toward the peak. "How about gettin' up there?"

The Apache led off and they fell into line. The slope became steeper, the climbing harder and the heat ferocious, boiling up from the rocks all around them. Johnson shot a look at Amita.

"I'm all right—just hot," she said; and they slogged on.

Up ahead Jaime held up a hand, climbed onto a boulder

and stood looking over the country spread below. He put several minutes into this study before he slid down and beckoned them on. Ten minutes later he stopped again. He had found them another level almost free of rocks. He called their attention to some bits of scattered charcoal. "Campsite—old, but not old enough. Maybe ten-twelve years." Amita found a couple of old and discolored buttons. Jaime found the broken blade of a knife while Johnson was examining the boulders along the edge of this flat.

"Don't ask me how," he muttered, scowling round, "but two of these smaller ones have been moved. A long time ago. There," he said, pointing, "is where they were moved from."

A good ten feet inside the campsite.

It was Johnson who found the rusted tin plate half-buried in the detritus. They did a lot more looking but nothing else turned up, and they went on. They chewed on jerky dug from Nugget's saddlebags. Johnson gave him a little water in his hat, then passed around the waterbag. There was a fringe of straggly bushes hanging on to the west edge of this flat and Nugget lunched on these.

Johnson said, "Wouldn't be a heap smart to let night catch us this far from camp." He was thinking about that lion Jaime'd heard. He had in mind also how easy it would be to get lost in this maze, or too far away to get back before dark.

They began climbing again, Jaime carrying his Winchester, Johnson sweatily hanging on to his single-shot Sharps. They were scarcely twenty feet from where the wind-whipped top of this climb leveled off when the lion's growl came from dead ahead.

Startled, each of them froze in their tracks, all but Nugget who, looking prickly with fright, huddled his head against Johnson's shoulder, silently shaking.

The lion wasn't in sight. He wasn't far off, either, scarcely a good leap away from the sound of that growling. Jaime worked the bowie from his belt. Through dry lips Johnson said, "Wait . . ." and flung a fist-sized rock up onto that sawed-off peak.

The lion roared and was suddenly in sight, poised on the lip with lashing tail, lips drawn back from his teeth in a snarl. Johnson fired from the hip with no time to aim, the sound of the Sharps drowning everything else as the lion, claws extended, went into the air.

EIGHT

As the dark shape came plummeting toward them and Johnson was yanking the girl from its path the Apache, crouched at point-blank range, slammed three Winchester slugs into it and only just missed being swept by its claws as the big cat landed, outstretched in death.

Johnson, later discussing the close call, said he could mighty near feel the grass waving over him. But all he managed at the moment was, "Dang if you ain't a pretty fair shot."

Jaime said, "Turns out all I did was gild the lily." Poking the lion with the toe of his boot he indicated where Johnson's shot had struck. "He'd about everything knocked out of him before I pulled trigger."

Amita, eyes still enormous, said shakily, "Be still, you two! Only reason you can talk is by God's grace," and she crossed herself with a kind of a shudder.

Both men nodded and turned away to catch their breath. With an arm round his neck Amita hung onto Nugget, visibly trembling as reaction took over.

Jaime eyed Johnson. "Shall we skin it?"

"No!" the girl cried. "You've killed it—leave it alone!"

Johnson and Jaime exchanged blank looks. Johnson shrugged, ejected the spent cartridge case and reloaded his buffalo gun. Women! he thought. There just wasn't no figuring them.

Jaime scrambled up to the place the lion had leaped from while Johnson stared down across the boulder-strewn east flank, already in shadow, to the heat-blurred desert far below. Ought to be starting back, he reckoned. Above him the sounds of the Apache poking about in his white man's boots turned Johnson's mind away from the girl to what had fetched him here in the first place.

Jaime called. "There's a hole here, all right."

Johnson climbed up to have a look.

He found the peak's sawed-off top measured about a quarter of a mile in circumference. "Been a camp here," Jaime said, looking round. "Swept clean by the winds but you can see the black scars of old fires. Plenty of animal bones. There's your hole," he said, pointing. "Lion's den, probably."

Johnson went over, "Yeah. Prob'ly." Still, he thought, it could have been the entrance to Eusibio's mine, covered over by the Indians, dug into recently by the lion. "Want to take a look?"

"Not me." Jaime grinned. "Might be a Mrs. Lion holed up in there." His glance went over the terrain once more. "Where'd they get the wood for their fires?"

"Trees here once. Guess they chopped them all down. Noticed a couple stumps scramblin' up here. Better come back tomorrow with a pick an' shovel. Gettin' late. We better move."

Back in camp at the glen with the pool Johnson gave Nugget the last of the oats and set about preparing something for the rest of them to eat, thinking as he did so they were not going to be able to stay here much longer with supplies running out and no fodder for the animals.

Amita with a bucket of water retired to her tent to clean herself up. Johnson shot a wistful look at the pool but reckoned, like the girl, they would have to make do with sponge baths from the bucket. Guessed he must be getting pretty whiffy already. If he'd been here by himself he'd have had a good swim. But there it was; people, like always, presented complications. If there was one thing they loved it was making rules for the rest of the tribe.

With supper over none of them showed much interest in sitting around. The girl went back in her tent and pulled the flap. The Apache went over to tend to his horses while Johnson scrubbed up the supper things. Then, joining Jaime under the cottonwoods, Johnson said, keeping his voice down, "I figure two more days'll just about do it. Once we're plumb out of grub we're goin' to be in a bind. Ain't a damn thing here fer them horses to eat and Nugget ain't going to be much better off."

Jaime nodded. "Don't reckon you white folks would be a heap partial to a diet of lizards and hoppers. We get down on the desert we can likely find enough rabbits to get by on. Still," he looked up with a grimace—"Mita's got her figuring plumb set on that mine."

"Yeah. Don't suppose there's any place within reach where we could stock up again an' come back here?"

"Used to be a cross trails store about twenty miles east. Trader's place. Might be there now but most likely not. Where you figuring to go if we pull out?"

"Good question," Johnson grumbled. "Better hit fer that store and hope it's still there."

They exchanged sober glances. "Reckon we could leave Amita in camp tomorrow?"

Jaime grinned. "Not without you tie her up."

"Yeah. Well," Johnson said, "I'm goin' to turn in."

They were up at first light. While they were eating their cut-down rations Johnson broached the subject of Amita remaining here to hold down the camp and could tell straightaway by the look on her face it was wasted breath. She had her chin up again and her back up, too. "Whose mine is this, anyway?" she sputtered. "If there's anything up there I want to see it for myself."

"Of course," Jaime soothed, and Johnson said, "We just kind of figured you might want to rest up."

The green eyes flashed. "You better figure again."

"Today and tomorrow," Johnson said bluntly, "is all we've got. We've got to git someplace we can find some more grub—can't see that any of us is fixed to eat gold, not even if we find it."

So they set off with Nugget for the top of the mountain. Knowing the way they made a little better time and reached the dead lion just short of ten o'clock, Johnson judged from a look at his shadow. The buzzards had been at work, a grim reminder of what could happen to all of them.

The hole at the top didn't look any different than it had yesterday. "Who's going to crawl in there?" Jaime asked, and Johnson grinned sourly.

"Don't reckon any of us is brash enough for that. First thing to do is widen this hole, enough anyway to see what's ahead of us." Hefting the pick he said, "I'll start it off."

They, the two men, spelled each other at ten-minute intervals while the girl held Jaime's rifle in case of sudden need. But no growls came up to them out of the hole and by the end of an hour it became plainly apparent there was nothing for them here. No shovel or pick marks beyond what they themselves had just made.

Jaime said, "Shall we try that other peak? The one with a hole full of rattlesnakes?"

Johnson rasped his stubbled chin. "I think that's a pleasure we'll reserve for another day." He looked at the girl. "My best notion for right now is to git down off this mountain and start huntin' for some grub." He could see that Amita disliked intensely the thought of leaving but she was practical enough to realize the alternative and reluctantly nodded.

They returned to the glen, packed up their gear, saddled the two horses and set off through the curling heat that by now was hot enough to fry an egg anyplace, and moved onto the smugglers' trail desert bound.

It was close to dark when they reached the desert floor. They could push on or spend the night and start off relatively fresh in the morning. Left to Amita, she voted to push on. The air was much cooler now and as they rode through the dark of the desert night Johnson, aboard Nugget, put Jaime on point to locate the old trading post he'd mentioned as a possible source of food. He was glad they'd thought to fill the waterbags because if that post wasn't being operated now, was burned down or abandoned, there was just no telling how far they'd have to go.

In the gray light of false dawn they glimpsed a huddle of low buildings about two miles ahead. "At least," Jaime said, "the place is still standing."

As they drew nearer they could see it was not only still there but inhabited. In the pole corrals several horses looked up to nicker at them. They rode up to the place— not without some sharp-eyed misgivings on the part of Johnson—dismounted and dropped their reins across the hitch pole. Jaime meandered through the open door, Amita following, anxious to get into some shade. Johnson, at the edge of the three steps giving onto the roofed verandah, paused to give his glance time to adjust to the dimness inside.

What he saw when he stepped in was a long counter ahead of him, above and behind it long rows of shelves packed with goods; but what he looked at longest was a pair of rannies in cowpuncher clothes lounging hipshot against it, conversation broken off to inspect the newcomers with hard narrowing stares.

"Thirsty weather," offered the man behind the counter, a thickset middle-aged gent in a sweat-stained shirt and galluses. "What can I do fer you? Pair of cold beers and a sody-pop fer the lady?"

"Cold beer sounds good to me," Jaime said. Amita said she would have beer too. The man looked at Johnson. "What's yours, friend?"

Johnson said, "Ain't seen you in a coon's age, Wolf. Kinda slow round here fer you, ain't it?"

"Reckon you taken me for somebody else," the man said, lifting two beers from a tub of water in which a few pieces of ice like lost souls were still floating. "Never set eyes on you in my life."

"See you later, Harry," one of the cowpunchers said, and jingled out of the place, followed by the other.

Johnson drifted over to the door, watching them ogle the pair of strange horses before climbing onto their own and taking off.

Coming back to the counter he said, "Got any groceries a feller could buy?"

"Some. You want canned stuff?"

"Ten cans of corned beef, five of tomatoes, three cans of squash, ten pounds of flour, box of salt, ten pounds of cornmeal, ten pounds of pinto beans and three cans of peaches."

When the man had finished stacking things on the counter he said, "That'll come to forty-two fifty."

Johnson dug out two twenty-dollar gold pieces, two silver dollars and a pair of quarters. Put them down beside his order. "An' a couple of burlaps to put this stuff in."

"I'll sack 'em," Jaime offered.

"Now," Johnson said, "I'll take one of them beers," and put three more two-bit pieces on the counter, all the time keeping one eye on the fellow.

Amita finished her beer just as Johnson finished his. Jaime hoisted one of the sacks and followed the girl out onto the verandah. Johnson picked up the other sack and went out after them without further words.

With the sacks, one on each side, securely anchored to the horn of his saddle, Jaime swung up and the others followed suit. Johnson led off as though they were headed for the Sulphur Springs Valley, and not till they'd put some scenery between themselves and the trading post did he turn left toward their mountain.

Jaime looked up at him curiously. "You acquainted with that joker?"

"Not to say 'acquainted' exactly. And maybe, like he said, I could be mixed up. But if he ain't Jed Wolf he's a dead ringer fer him. Feller used to hang out at Charleston. Worked at the stamp mill daytimes. Nights he worked up a flourishin' business stoppin' stages that come out of Tombstone."

"I know this much," Jaime said, looking thoughtful. "He wasn't running that post when I was here."

"Those two fellers that left ahead of us took a good long look at the brand of your horses. If I see 'em again I'll shoot first an' talk later."

NINE

They stopped a couple times to rest and give the two horses and Nugget a few swallows of water. Johnson thought Amita looked a mite tuckered so when they got to what he figured was about halfway he pulled Nugget up and allowed it would be plumb foolish to wear out their animals. It wasn't the best place for a campsite, being right out in the open, but he told Jamie to put up the tent. "We won't bother with grub—we kin eat when we get to the mountain."

Jamie gave him a long look but put up the tent without comment.

After the girl had gone into it Johnson took the Apache aside. "I want to give them hombres a chance to catch up."

"You think they're trailin' us?"

"I saw a couple dusts. Might not mean a thing," Johnson said, "But if there's one thing we don't want on that mountain it's company. Better to have it out with them on our own terms."

Jamie nodded. Johnson said, "How do you feel about robbin' that store?"

"When?"

"Sometime durin' the night when your horses are more up to it. We forgot to pick up any feed. If these critters play out—even one by one, we're like to be keepin' old Eusibio company."

When Jamie, it seemed like, was not too enthusiastic, Johnson said, "Hell, I'll go if it's ag'in' your religion— guess we'd better grab fifty pounds anyway."

Jamie chuckled. "You'd have made a good Injun."

"I look at it this way," Johnson said. "If them fellers was honest they wouldn't be follerin', and if they're hooked up with that Harry they're about as crooked as a snake in a cactus patch."

"I've been thinkin'," Jamie grunted. "If Grue and company are on our trail what's to prevent them seein' our rockpile—?"

"First place, not havin' our part of the map there ain't nothing to key 'em into it. Top of that, I doubt they know a darn thing about mines or what sort of country to hunt them in. There's just two ways fer them to come onto us— finding someone who's seen the pair of you or follerin' your sign. And that's a powerful far piece to hang on to a set of tracks."

"Then if you're right we've lost them."

"Don't think I'd gamble on that," said Johnson, shaking his head. "If they run into those galoots we saw at that store they'd have a pretty good lead. Might even hire 'em. Seems I've heard someplace birds of a feather will flock together."

"That one of those paleface sayings?" Jamie asked.

"Yep—saw fer every occasion. Better be catchin' yourself a few winks," Johnson told him. "I'll be keeping my ears skinned out there in the brush. You hear anyone slippin' up on this camp just bounce a few slugs off the ground out in front of 'em. That'll shunt 'em towards me so I kin get in my licks—"

"You figuring to kill them?"

"Cripple them."

"When us Apaches have an enemy it ain't our way to postpone the inevitable."

"Reckon that's because you're bustin' to count coup. All we want is to be rid of them buggers. Bustin' a leg or a kneecap'll get 'em out of our hair just as good as a funeral. Don't always pay to be a hog in this business."

With a nod for his burro Johnson went striding off into the night and Nugget, blowing softly through his nose, reluctantly followed.

Off and on, when not too pressed with things of more consequence, Johnson had been doing considerable thinking about red hair and two come-hither eyes all a-sparkle like a pair of bright emeralds. Not ready to admit the girl had got her hooks into him, he couldn't help admiring her pluck and endurance. Never afraid to speak her mind, eager, exciting as a Thoroughbred filly and just as shy though she tried not to show it. There was something about her he hadn't found in other females, something he reckoned she must have got from her gypsy mother. Skin the color of melted honey . . .

Made him pull himself up more than once, thinking that way. In the rough life he led, off alone in far places, he'd no place for a woman except round a campfire when he sometimes sat dreaming with the coyotes yapping from some distant hill. But when he saw her and Jamie with their heads close together the quick resentment boiling up in him was warning enough he'd better watch his step. As he'd harshly reminded himself on such occasions Teluride Johnson wasn't the marrying kind. He didn't want no woman complicating his life.

Sitting out in the brush with his Sharps and his burro, the one critter he could trust, Johnson shook his head and tried to stay awake. He'd better stop thinking about her, by godfries, before he found himself with the grass waving over him!

Say what you would she looked a pretty good armful, the kind of a female a man would like to come home to, someone to chase the long shadows from his mind and make him feel wanted.

Then, of a sudden, he was sitting bolt upright, listening into a night that had no sound of crickets.

The abrupt explosions of a Winchester firing brought him onto his feet, crouched and ready, slitted glance swiveling round sharp as a knife blade. There was no moon, yet as always in desert country there was that strange luminous quality that allowed a man bred into it to see like a cat, and his ears picked up the pound of hard-running hoofs rushing straight toward him.

When you've got but one shot to throw into a fracas a man learns to make it count. And so it was with Johnson, holding back with edgy patience, buffalo gun clamped hard against shoulder, waiting out the seconds to make sure he wouldn't miss. He could see them now, two of them just as he'd expected, low crouched above the wind-flurried manes of their stretched-out ponies.

Closer, damn you—closer! This was wasted energy without he smashed both.

He couldn't see the whites of their eyes in the dark, just the pale blobs of faces when with infinite care he squeezed off his shot. Even through the blast of the Sharps he heard a wild cry, saw the shape come erect with a lurch in the saddle as he dropped the rifle, palming his six-shooter, firing twice as they raced away, the second man with both hands clamped to the horn.

Calling Nugget he started back to camp.

"How'd it go?" Jamie's voice, cool as frog legs.

"Think I got both of them."

"Reckon they'll be back?"

"Not them. That Harry might come snoopin' around. You better get started," Johnson growled, still tight-pinched by the violence he'd loosed. "I can take care of Harry if he shows. Just make sure he don't take care of you."

He saw Amita back of the Apache, eyes big as saucers. "Where's he going?"

"Back to the store. We forgot the horse feed. Got to have it."

Jamie laughed. "Nothing to worry about," he said, patting her shoulder.

Johnson's lips tightened as he looked after Jamie, watched him get on his horse. Amita said, "When I was a young one I dreamed of great adventures, going places, seeing things, everything rosy and sparkling and bright. Now I don't know. Would you call this an adventure?"

Johnson shrugged. "Reckon some people would."

"I don't think it's much like those things I dreamed of."

"Dreams don't have much in common with facts," said Johnson gruffly. "You better get some rest. Tomorrow I figure to be back on that mountain."

"Maybe," she said, "we should give up this search—I didn't know there'd be shooting."

He thought she looked sort of wistful. The only thing he could think of to say was, "He'll be all right. He's got his head screwed on straight," and thought she seemed a bit odd, staring at him, before she bade him good night and ducked into her tent, pulling the flap into place.

TEN

The sun was an hour high when Nugget impatiently nudged him awake. Johnson, throwing off the blanket, sat groggily up and, scrubbing the sleep from his eyes, got his feet under him and staggered erect. The tent was still closed. The girl's horse was nickering, crow-hopping about in its hobbles. Following its look Johnson saw Jaime quartering the brush where the visitors had been at the time of the shooting. "You git that grain?"

"You bet," Jamie called and fetched his horse into camp, Johnson lifting off the fifty pounds of oats.

"Have any trouble?"

"Nope. Just helped myself. That Harry snores like he's got rollers in his nose. How's things been here?"

"Fine as silk. I'll rustle up some breakfast while you feed an' water these critters."

First thing he did once he got his fire going was to put on a pot of water for the coffee. The Apache had managed to fetch six eggs, which Johnson fried with real enthusiasm and served with cornbread made in the same skillet.

Then he dropped a few coffee beans into the pot and yelled to Amita to come and get it.

While they were eating Amita said, "When I was a little girl I used to dream that a handsome knight in shining armor would someday come to carry me off on his beautiful white charger."

"What I used to dream," Johnson confessed, "was that my old man would get enough cash money ahead—this was mainly on cold nights or during a blizzard—to buy us a inside water closet."

Jaime laughed. "I used to have them kind of dreams too, only in mine it was the Great White Father up in Washington would do it."

Soon as they'd consumed all the food he'd fried up Johnson said they'd better get packed and be on their way.

Two hours later they were climbing the smugglers' trail once again. Jamie said, "I looked around out there. Reckon you hit both of them. Doubt if they'll be round here again."

Amita looked at Johnson but kept her lip hobbled.

He said, "Just bloodied 'em up a little. Give them time to consider the error of their ways."

She let out a sigh but managed a smile. "Are you always that impulsive?"

"Well . . . no," he answered after thinking about it. "Sometimes I'm more so."

It was a hot, tiring climb and all of an hour later before they rounded the towerlike butte and came into the glen with its welcoming shade and that bright pool of clear water. Everyone breathed a sigh of relief. It was kind of like coming home, Johnson thought. Even the girl perked up as the two men unpacked and put away the supplies, and Nugget rolled on the grass and shook himself and then trotted over to get himself a drink. Jamie led the two horses to the pool then whisked them away from it before they were satisfied. "You can have some more." he said, "after you've cooled off."

Then Amita said to Johnson, "What do you have in mind for tomorrow?"

"Reckon we better tackle that rattlesnake peak. Jamie

remembers a hole up there which just might lead to your uncle's mine.''

"Ugh," she said, wrinkling her nose in a very fetching manner. "I believe I'll stay here."

The Apache put up her tent and, after Amita had gone into it, drew Johnson aside to say, "Wonder if that's such a good idea. Supposing old Harry decides to pay us a visit?"

Johnson pushed that around in his head. "He don't look like a tracker. After he learns what happened to those sports he sent after us I don't think he'll feel up to it. You want to stay here an' wait fer him?"

"No, thanks. I'm a real snake lover. Being knee deep in them is one of my hobbies."

Johnson gave him the edge of a grin. "You can't stand havin' me hog all the fun."

Jamie grinned, too. "I like to be where the action is."

So they fed the two horses and Nugget a good ration of oats, lazed around for a while, had a good supper with peaches to top it off and went early to bed.

Next morning after eating and while the sun hadn't yet got over the rimrocks the two men, both riding horses and supplied with a pick and shovel in addition to their rifles, set off for what Jamie called Rattlesnake Peak.

They tried to shortcut across the flank of the mountain and were both surprised to discover what appeared to be a goat trail leading with various wriggles almost straight to their objective, which they reached well short of noon; in fact, barely ten-thirty by Johnson's estimate after a glance at his shadow. A further astonishment came their way when they found no snakes around the hole Jamie had mentioned.

"Sure looks like a mine tunnel," Johnson remarked, carefully examining the entrance, "and not worked in a good while. You want to go first?"

"Hate to take that pleasure away from you—"

"You found it. Go ahead." Johnson grinned. So, carrying the shovel and Winchester, Jamie led the way into the tunnel.

"Odd," he said, "them Indians never bothered to close it," and Johnson, carrying the pick, grimly nodded. "Either the mine's played out or Eusibio got into borasca and the Injuns got him before he was able to find the vein again."

They went into the mountain for perhaps an eighth of a mile before the tunnel swung left and they no longer had any light from the entrance. Jamie said, "We're going to have to fix up some kind of a torch."

"Yeah. Guess you've noticed," Johnson grumbled, "there ain't been a trace of color so far. No timbers, either. Go and fix up a torch. I'll wait for you here."

It certainly had Johnson fighting his hat to figure why anyone would have driven a tunnel this deep without a trace of ore. The only answer he could come up with was that the diggers had been following a pretty narrow vein. When Jamie returned with a greasewood torch they moved round the bend to find more of the same. "Not a goddam trace of color," Johnson growled. "And no dump out there. What in hell did they do with the dirt they dug out of here?"

Jamie shrugged. "Beats me."

"It don't make sense."

"In forty years what they took out would have pretty much settled, grown over maybe."

"Maybe," Johnson muttered. He looked hard at his companion. "You know what I think? I figure we come in through the exit. We'll be findin' that dump at the other end. Let's shove on."

The tunnel took another twist, began going downhill and now they saw timbers made into brackets to hold up the roof. "Wood's well preserved," Johnson noted. "Here—hold on a second," he growled, examining the wall. "They took ore outa here," he said, pointing.

"Don't look much like that specimen."

"This is where she petered out," Johnson said, all fired up again, and moved along, examining both walls. After another hundred feet they came to an adit, a shaft driven into the right-hand wall. They found ore in both walls as they moved along the path of the adit. They were also discovering traces of damp. "Springs above here some-place," Johnson growled, beginning to look concerned. But the ore in place looked more like the sample Amita had shown them. Then, abruptly, the tunnel widened out into a fair-sized room.

"Must've hit on a real bonanza here," Johnson muttered, looking around. "There's a lot of high-grade still left in these walls."

"I wonder," Jamie said, "where we're getting the air from."

Johnson thought about that. "How far in do you reckon we've come?"

"At a guess I'd say about twelve to fifteen hundred feet. Pretty far to get air from where we came into this."

Johnson blew out a breath. "Let's go on to the end of this adit," he said, leading off. "Notice the formation. We're right into the quartz now."

Jaime nodded. "Getting wetter, too, and they've run out of timber."

The tunnel angled again and a hundred feet beyond this bend the passage was blocked where a great batch of rock had come down from the roof. Johnson, poking about in the rubble, held up a fist-sized chunk of quartz. They looked at each other. The piece he held out was a dead ringer for the chunk Amita had brought from Villalobos.

Johnson shoved the piece of rock in his pocket. "Come on. We better hike for the main tunnel before we run outa light."

ELEVEN

When they emerged onto the ledge from what they'd supposed was the tunnel entrance Johnson said, "I wish we'd
found that other opening."

"We'd probably still be stumbling around in the dark—
might have taken a header and gone halfway to hell."

"Might've found one of those springs. We'll take another look tomorrow. Be smarter I guess to move camp
up here. Runnin' back and forth every day ain't my idea
of eco-nomical. We've grub for another six days if we're
careful. I can't see usin' up half our time travelin'."

"You're the prospector," Jaime said. "but there's
something about that place I can't like. Don't know what—
just a feelin' I've got."

"Reckon it started when you noticed we were still gettin' air. I got a notion about that. I think it was coming in
from that place where the ceilin' dropped."

"Suppose we're back in there and some more of it
comes down. Between us and the main tunnel?"

"Be a real laugh," Johnson said, grinning. "Might get
to meet Eusibio."

It was not yet dark when they got back to the glen. Nugget gave them a skreaky pumphandle greeting with his lip curled back, and Amita wanted to know what they'd found, if anything.

"Guess we found your uncle's mine," Johnson replied, "but Jaime don't like it."

The green eyes swung to the Apache. "Why don't you like it?"

Jaime shrugged. "Call it a hunch. Be mighty easy, I think, to get buried in that place. There's already been one rockfall."

She brought her look back to Johnson. "Do you think it's been worked since the last time my uncle was here?"

"Didn't see any sign. But there's somethin' funny about that place. The hole we went into, thinking that was the entrance, went near half a mile before we came onto the first sign of ore. They drove a tunnel you can stand in all that way through dirt an' country rock before they got to the quartz. It just ain't natural. Only explanation I can hit on is we must have gone in by the exit. But if that's the answer you got to wonder why didn't they go out the way they came in."

"Perhaps," Amita said, frowning, "they couldn't. Perhaps the Indians had sealed off the entrance . . ."

Jaime said grimly, "I'll bet that's it!"

"Or," said Amita. "they might have been trapped by another rockfall."

"And the way we went in was the way they dug out?" Johnson said. "I can't buy that. First place, and without much air, they wouldn't have made their tunnel that big. All they'd have needed was a hole they could crawl through. And beyond all that, they moved a powerful lot of dirt. What happened to it? We didn't find any dump."

While she was trying to get around this, Jaime said, "He wants us to move this camp up there. We found some damp places but no water you can drink, and what would we do with the burro and horses?"

"Why don't we sleep on it?" Johnson said.

So they left it at that. Amita having already fed and watered the animals, Johnson got a fire going and set about fixing supper. "Should've got some spuds to bake in the ashes." Then he said to the girl, "You notice anyone prowlin' round down below?"

She faced him, eyes widening, shaking her head. "Were you thinking of Grue?"

"That storekeeper mostly. I don't imagine Grue has caught up with us . . . yet. We should have done something about our tracks while we were down there," he said. "Anyone takin' the trouble to look could see straightaway this trail has been traveled. We better take care of that tomorrow."

Amita said uneasily, "Do you think Grue will find us?"

"Expect that'll depend on how anxious he is. If he can track you to that spring we started off from, which don't seem exactly reasonable, he won't have too much trouble follerin' us to this mountain, I wouldn't think. What we better watch out for is that feller at the tradin' post."

Jaime said, "I'll take care of those tracks first thing in the morning."

But a freak thunderstorm came up during the night, a real gully-washing downpour. Johnson said he felt like he was about to sprout fins and the Apache told Amita—who was already soaked from water flowing under the tent— that he wished they had thought to fetch a canoe. "Not much use in going down there now," he said, and Johnson agreed. "Darn lucky we been keepin' our supplies in a tarp."

"Perhaps we *should* move camp," Amita said as they stood shivering under the dripping trees. "Can we take the animals into that tunnel?"

"Sure," Johnson said. "There's a kind of room hollowed out where those old boys got the bulk of their gold from. How much did your uncle fetch back to Villalobos?"

"Papa told me once all the gold he ever saw from Eusibio's mine was what he had fetched in a little sample sack. The piece I showed you came out of that sack. Papa wouldn't believe he had any mine; said what he'd showed round was Lost Dutchman samples he'd got from the bank.''

"He had a mine," Johnson said. "You're going to see it this morning. And, speakin' of banks, some bank may be holding the gold from all that ore they took out. Here's a chunk I brought back for you—picked it out of that rock-fall.''

Amita's eyes got big and showed her excitement. She ducked into the tent and returned with a fist-size piece of ore in each hand. She laughed at their expressions. Both chunks had plainly come from the same place.

She said with eyes sparkling, "Let's move the camp up there.''

It was going on eight o'clock when they left the glen. The route taken by Jaime and Johnson yesterday was still passable because the ground underfoot was mostly shale, but in three or four places the storm had cut gullies which had to be negotiated with considerable care. Because of this the morning was more than half-gone before they reached their destination and Johnson, during the journey, had swept many a searching glance across the rock-strewn slopes and what he could see of the desert below. Without, however, catching the least sign of movement.

Since leaving here yesterday he'd done a great deal of thinking. The size and length of that near half mile of untimbered tunnel in which the walls had shown neither quartz nor gold continued to nag at him. Why had it been dug? And why so large? And where was the dirt they had taken out of it? Around this hole, not seen from below, there was waist-high brush obviously grown since Eusibio had been here, bearing out Jaime's suggestion. All that dirt could have been dumped right here. Forty years of rain and winds might easily have eroded much of this. Indeed, around them now could be seen the tops of half-buried rocks beneath the brush growing over them.

It occurred to Johnson as he studied this slope there might well have been another reason for the size and length of this apparently foolish half mile of digging. He tried this notion out on the others.

"Suppose," he said, "them Injuns—thinking they had

Eusibio an' company neatly bottled—had sealed up the original entrance. Now suppose the ore in that original tunnel had all been dug out and that Eusibio's boys had been working that adit. If he knew about where it was in conjunction with the surface he could have driven this tunnel right here to git back to it . . .''

"Then he must have been pretty stupid," Jaime growled. "A sensible man would have got right over it and sunk a shaft. Way I figure they couldn't have been more than forty feet above it, maybe less."

"Perhaps," Amita offered, "there was solid rock above it." She said, warming up to this, "Maybe they tried and couldn't get through it."

Jaime gave her a patronizing smile and, reaching out, a pat on the shoulder. "You're forgetting that cave-in. That never come from no solid rock."

Johnson said, "We kin spare a half hour. Let's have a look."

So, leaving Amita to hold their animals, Johnson and Jaime climbing over the hole began working their way up the rock-strewn slope and presently came on a jagged hole like a poorly dug well that was now half-full of rain water. "An' there's another," Johnson said, pointing. Jaime, scowling, loosed a ten-pound rock from the surrounding debris and dropped it into this second hole. They heard it hit bottom with a solid thump. "There's your answer," Johnson said, and went back to heave another rock into the first hole with the same result. "Prob'ly a ledge—granite by the sound of it."

They went back to Amita. "Two holes," Johnson said. "They hit solid rock in both of them."

"Then why didn't they tackle the original entrance? The one you figure was blocked by Apaches?" Jaime muttered.

Johnson shrugged. "Reckon they must've had a good reason." Looking around, he said, "Let's git on with it," and dug a carbide lantern from the supplies on Nugget.

Leading the animals, they entered the tunnel. The two horses didn't much care for it and had to be tugged until Johnson thought to slip a rope under their tails. When they reached the first bend Johnson tipped a bit of moisture into his lantern from one of the waterbags and touched a match to the gas. With this lighting their way they pressed on, Amita exclaiming now and again about the amount of energy expended in the creation of this passage.

"This here is the adit where it seems they must have been getting most of the ore from," Johnson explained, leading off down this corridor with its timbered walls. When they reached the room-sized wide place, its walls glistening with gold-streaked quartz, her eyes turned bright with excitement. It looked a lot like a cavern but without stalactites, though a couple columns had been left to help support the timbered roof. The place was roughly thirty by forty feet.

"We'll leave the horses and supplies right here," Johnson said, unpacking the animals while Jaime was hitching their reins to one of the columns. "Here—don't tie 'em there," Johnson rapped. "You tie 'em up and they panic they could rip them columns right outa there. Just leave them on dropped reins."

When the supplies were unpacked and the saddles removed he said, "Now we'll go back to the main tunnel and see what's at the other end of it."

This did not take as long as anticipated. Leaving the adit, they had not progressed much more than a hundred feet through several mild bends before they came to where the passage was choked tight with fallen rock. "Looks like you were right," Jaime said.

"You think this was the original entrance?" Amita asked.

Johnson nodded. "Just beyond here someplace. Eusibio probably left his blasting equipment just far enough inside to keep it dry and them Injuns used it. No tellin' how many tons of rock they brought down."

"Let's go back," Jaime said, looking about him uneasily.

When they got back to where they'd left their animals, Johnson said, "Come on, let's take another look at this blocked passage."

When they reached the rockfall they'd been stopped by

yesterday they found the debris pretty wet and puddles on the floor this side of it. "Right again," Jaime admitted. "Up there's where the air came from all right. Must be some fairly large cracks in the overhead to let this much water in. So, if the rest of your figuring turns out to be right, why didn't Eusibio drive a shaft here?"

"Prob'ly couldn't find the cracks," Johnson answered. "Maybe he didn't come this far. From up on the mountain it ain't easy to judge what's below you from memory. Might of been Injuns up there."

Amita asked, "What is the next thing?"

"The next thing," Johnson said, "is to go back to where we got into this mountain an' make damn sure we're not leaving any tracks to be looked at!"

"I don't like it," Jaime said. "I get a bad feeling in this place."

"Chindis?" Johnson said with a grin. "You figure the spirits of the dead have settled in here?"

"I just don't like it," Jaime growled. "You can laugh if you want, but common sense tells me we could almighty easy be trapped in here like your uncle was," he told Amita with his face looking gray beneath his built-in tan.

Johnson snorted. "It's that Harry we got to watch out for. Dead men I kin take in my stride. Any spirits round here have been forty years dead!"

TWELVE

But what with all this gab about rockfalls and dead people it wasn't hard to see that considerable of Amita's initial enthusiasm had departed. She looked, Johnson thought, both nervous and more than just a little upset. He said to Jaime, "Get out there and do somethin' about those tracks. If you can't stomach this place stay out there and keep watch."

"I'll take care of the tracks," Jaime answered, face darkening, "but when guts were passed out I got as much as anyone. If you're staying here I'll stay here too."

"Atta boy," Johnson said. "Now you're talkin'."

Since they had but the one lamp, and nothing down there a torch could be made of, both Amita and Johnson accompanied the Apache back to what they had thought was the entrance. They couldn't think where the time had gone. Here it was evening already with the shadows stretched long across the rocks below.

While Jaime was busy obliterating tracks Johnson was examining all that could be seen of the surrounding country, giving particular attention to the lower rocks where someone might be seeking to find a way up, but he found nothing to be concerned about, no sign of intruders, no least motion but a thin haze of dust from wind sweeping up off the desert. He watched this awhile through crinched-up eyes but there were no riders in it.

Jaime, farther out, had started several false trails, steering them off through the brush where he'd let them fade away. And now he was backing toward the ledge where Johnson and Amita stood watching, brushing out all sign as he moved nearer. Backing onto the ledge he said, "That ought to do it."

They all walked back into the tunnel then, moving on to the place where they'd left the animals. Nothing had changed. The horses pricked up their ears, one of them softly whinnying. Nugget rubbed his nose against Johnson's shoulder, and Amita said, "I'm hungry." Which was when Johnson realized they'd nothing to build a fire with. Under his breath he used a few words not fit for female ears. "I'll have to go back," he said, disgusted. "Can't cook without—"

Amita said, "We've three cans of tomatoes. We could each have one. Don't go back now."

And Jaime said, "I don't much fancy waitin' here in the dark."

"Keep the light," Johnson said, handing the lamp to the girl. "I been through there enough to do it with my eyes shut," and off he went.

"How could we ever have forgotten the fire?"

"Expect," Jaime said, "our minds were on other things. I'll water the animals and give them some oats."

She said, "Do you really think my uncle was here all those years ago?"

"He just about had to be, judging by the chunk of ore Johnson picked out of that rockfall. Same formation and quality as the one you brought from Villalobos."

"I wonder what they're doing back there."

"Same as always, I imagine. All the hubbub stirred up when we took off has likely died down by this time. Haddam, if he's there, will keep himself busy filling his pockets and doctoring the accounts—"

They heard steps in the passage and Johnson came in with a big armful of brush which he dropped in a corner.

"Rub out your sign?" Jaime asked.

Johnson nodded. "Did better'n that. Stood up some brush in front of that hole." But it sure did get his bristles up seeing them two with their heads together.

As he broke up a few sticks to get supper with—driest ones he could get his hands on because cooped in here with its limited air only a fool would add smoke to his problems—he reminded himself of course they'd be friendly, knowing each other for most of her life.

Building air castles—and him a grown man—was the mark of a nump who didn't have all his marbles. She wasn't for him or no damn Injun either, brought up as she'd been in the lap of luxury, her old man a *rico* of considerable importance with more folks serving him than lived in this whole territory. It was time he got a hold on himself!

"Found a couple things out there," he mentioned. "Another skull with its head smashed in, an' this," he said, putting a weight of tarnished silver into her hand.

Her eyes grew big in the pallor of her cheeks as she stood there staring down at the thing, not wanting to believe it but believing anyway. "Uncle Eusibio's watch!" she cried.

Alongside a spring in the shadow of three great cottonwoods Brusco Melindroso watched Brodie Grue irascibly glaring at the crumpled piece of map as he'd been doing every evening for the past three weeks. Not one feature marked on that paper had they been able to find. Indeed without their Yaqui tracker they'd have run out of sign long since. Each day as they'd left Sonora farther behind it had become more and more difficult to follow the fugitives' tracks. Only the Villalobos brand stamped into the left-front shoe of Amita's horse had been responsible for getting them this far.

Melindroso, picked by Haddam after the death of the old majordomo, to boss the Villalobos vaqueros, bitterly cursed the day he'd been told by the lawyer to accompany

Grue on this miserable chase, having early learned his finicky notions did not sit well with this crazy gringo.

Because he was in mortal terror of the man he'd been keeping his mouth tightly shut ever since the day Grue had viciously kicked the old don's horse in the belly and come within an inch of smashing the animal's teeth with the barrel of his pistol. For his intervention that time Melindroso had been knocked down with a blow from that same pistol barrel. "When I want any yap outa you I'll ask for it!" Grue had yelled, glaring down at him malevolently.

Now, nervously watching the man, the Villalobos foreman dreadfully wondered where all this would end, and shuddered at the horrible thought of the fate awaiting the girl should Grue catch up with her.

The Yaqui refilled their waterbags from the spring before setting out on the following morning while it was yet hardly light enough to read sign. Each day the fugitives' tracks had been harder to follow, taken longer to sort out, feeding that crazy gringo's temper until even the Yaqui went in fear of his life.

By midafternoon the winds sporadically sweeping the desert had all but obliterated the faded tracks. Back at the spring Grue had noted the new set of tracks moving off with those of his quarry; his face had turned nearly black with rage. "Is this feller follerin' them tracks?" he'd demanded.

"But no, señor," said the Yaqui, trembling. "This new horse goes with them." He'd got down to study them even more closely. "These tracks all same age."

They camped that night beside the black scar of the fugitives' fire and were awakened long hours short of morning by a storm swept upon them without warning. They had gone to sleep beneath a sky filled with stars and were wakened soaking wet in the midst of a cloudburst which lasted even less than an hour. There were no tracks to be found in the morning light. Grue raged like a madman.

"How could you possibly know?" demanded Jaime. "You weren't even born when Eusibio died."

"I would know that watch anywhere. Mama had a tintype of Eusibio looking at his timepiece—that was what he called it. Mama told me often enough how he valued that watch. It was a present to him from Porfirio Díaz—see," she cried, rubbing it vigorously on the cloth of her riding skirt, "there is the Díaz family insignia!"

"Well, I guess that settles it," Johnson said. "The Apaches got all of them." He said to Amita, "Would you have any pictures of your mother? Your father?"

"Only the one. It was taken when they married. I have it in my room at the hacienda. She was ever so much prettier than me—a great beauty, everyone said. Papa once told me she was the toast of Guadalajara." She looked at him wistfully.

After they'd eaten and he'd cleaned up after the animals he put out his lamp to save carbide, spread out his blanket on the hard floor and stretched out to get whatever sleep fate allowed him, leaving the others to do whatever suited them.

Nugget, good as an alarm clock, nudged him awake at about five-thirty and followed him back through the passages to have a first look at whatever was stirring. All they saw was a ground squirrel and one lone buzzard sailing the air currents high above. No sign of prowlers.

Back with the others, both of whom still slept, he fed and watered Nugget and the horses, got a tiny fire going, threw some dough in the skillet and growled, "Com an' git it." They each ate two griddlecakes, downed with plain water.

Then he picked up the shovel and was heading for the rockfall when Amita called, "I'm going with you."

One thing he had done before starting breakfast was put more carbide into his lamp. With reluctance Jaime plunged after them. When they reached the place where the passage was blocked Johnson, setting down his lamp, picked up his shovel and began digging into the rockfall. Inside of ten minutes he'd dug out ten chunks of ore, good high-grade samples. "You're not going to try to move all that, are you?" Amita asked.

"Nope. Just want to see if the quality holds up," he

answered, going on with his shoveling. In the next half hour he got out eight more chunks, equally good. "Eusibio," he said, "was really onto somethin'. It will certainly pay to mine this, but it will take more hands and a mule train to fetch this stuff to where it can be smelted."

"Where'll we get the mules?" Jaime wanted to know.

"You know this country better'n I do. What's the nearest fair-sized town?"

"Nogales, I reckon. A long haul," Jaime said. "We just going to leave it while we go hunting mules?"

"Unless you want to stick around to keep an eye on it." Johnson scrubbed a fist along his jaw. "It ain't just the mules. We got to hire a crew, get a few sticks of dynamite, more picks an' shovels, a wheelbarrow, some rope and some crowbars. And canvas sacks. Gettin' the right sort of crew is the tough part."

"Isn't there any way we could leave out the crew and do it ourselves?" the girl asked.

"Sure. But it would mean putting in a lot more time here. We go sashayin' out of here with ten-twelve mules loaded down with this kind of ore we'll be a target for every crook between this place and Villalobos." He leaned on the shovel. "We'll need at least five men and the tougher the better. They don't have to be miners, but they'll have to have guts an' be able to hit what they shoot at."

"And what's to prevent them from shooting us?" Jaime growled.

Johnson grinned. "This," he said, and slapped his holstered pistol.

THIRTEEN

Jaime said incredulously, "One against five?"

"You'll be there, won't you?"

"Well . . . yes, but—"

"You're gettin' soft, Jaime. Too much education. If you'll be ready to pick off one of 'em I kin handle three and the other galoot will dig for the timbers. No problem."

With the girl looking on, hearing this talk, Jaime decided to rethink his notions. When Johnson got that look in his eye the Apache was reminded of what had happened to that pair from the trading post and decided it was time to hobble his lip.

Amita wasn't worried. There might be things about Johnson she'd prefer to see changed, but one thing she felt sure of. She would always be safe so long as he was in reach. She said, "When do we leave?"

"I'd like to booby-trap this place before we pull out. Trouble is, we haven't got anything to do it with," he said regretful-like. "Sooner we go the sooner we'll be back. Once we get to work here we'll have to fix a place for the

animals outside. And we'll need a few barrels to hold a
store of water; can't be takin' 'em to that pool every day.
And before we leave we'll have to top off these waterbags.
Guess we'll have to spend another day here.''

"I could go over there and get them filled now," she
said.

Johnson, considering that, finally shook his head.

"I'll go," Jaime offered.

"You'll have to leave tracks."

"Brush them out coming back."

Johnson thought about it some more and presently nodded. They all had a drink and gave each of the animals
enough to wet their whistles. Jaime saddled one of the
horses, slipped a bridle over its head, gathered up the waterbags, two of which were just about empty; leading his
horse he headed for the main tunnel, Johnson and the girl
going along to light his way.

After he had gone they sat down to watch his progress.
Amita said, "I can hardly believe we've actually found
Eusibio's mine. Does it seem that way to you?"

"Well, yes and no," Johnson admitted. "Of course
we've had a great deal of luck. Ever since quittin' the
Hashknife I've been huntin' lost mines. And in all that
time I've only found two, neither of 'em worth writin'
home about. But it stood to reason if the padre had a mine
and we looked long enough, sooner or later we were bound
to stumble onto it."

"It almost seems a miracle to me." She smiled.

Watching the Apache picking his way through those
boulders Johnson pulled his head around to peer down the
slopes and look across the desert, abruptly stiffening. Away
off there in the heat haze, seeming hardly bigger than dogs
at this distance, he saw three horsemen slogging along as
though they had all the time in the world. "Oh!" cried
Amita, following his look. "Who are they—can you tell?"

"Not from here . . . not yet, anyway. Seems like they're
moving from the direction of that store—comin' from
Harry with love, I expect. Let's see if they're aiming to
pay us a visit."

He didn't, she thought, sound the least bit alarmed, or even mildly excited.

"First, if they head this way, we'll give them a chance to show their intentions," he said. "If they keep on comin' after I wave them off we'll have to do something else."

The horsemen were near enough now that he could see the rifles tucked under their left legs . . . probably Winchester repeaters. An excellent firearm but lacking the range of the single-shot Sharps, the rifle most favored by buffalo hunters. "Look at that middle one—" She caught at his arm. "Isn't that Harry?"

Johnson nodded. "Sure does resemble him. Now we'll see," he said as though to himself. "They're wheelin' towards us. Havin' wasted a pair sendin' two boys to do a man's work he's comin' himself, figurin' to do better."

The trio were dismounting at the edge of the rocks. Cupping hands about mouth Johnson yelled down to them: "This mountain's private property—stay clear!" And heard his words banging round like bullets to which the three below paid not the least attention. Separating now, fanning out, rifles in hand, they were moving into the rocks. Amita seemed nervous. "What will we do?"

"We'll do what comes natural," Johnson assured her. "They been warned. You're lookin', Amita, at the kinda skunk that won't work for a livin', the have-nots that figure those what have got no rights to it. This here's our castle, we're goin' to protect it. Just set back an' relax."

Harry—probably Jed Wolf—had to Johnson's remembrance a long life of crime behind him, taking things from others and getting away with it. This time, he thought, you've picked the wrong coon.

The intruders, working between rocks, were now scarcely more than four hundred yards from where he sat with Amita nervously hovering over his shoulder.

Johnson lifted the Sharps.

"Far enough," he called, but they paid no attention.

Waiting a few moments Johnson squeezed off a shot.

The man at the far left with outflung arms was slammed by the impact against the boulder behind him, hung there an instant, then slid out of sight. The other pair, shocked, hastily dropped out of view.

Johnson told Amita to get into the tunnel.

"And what about you?" she protested.

"Got to give 'em a target. They'll clear out pretty quick."

He reloaded the Sharps. And sat there, waiting.

Harry stayed out of sight but the other man popped up his head for a look and Johnson knocked off a chunk of rock right beside it. The man, like a jackrabbit, took to his heels making far-apart tracks. Johnson reloaded. It was Harry he wanted. But Harry kept out of sight, little squiggles of dust marking the line of his retreat.

Johnson put another slug down there, making it ricochet off the rock ahead of Harry, giving the rascal something to think about. The man's still-alive crony had nearly reached the desert floor and their three whinnying ground-anchored mounts when Jaime rode into view less than a hundred yards away. The Apache flung up his rifle, flame streaking from its barrel. The man lurched and staggered, fright driving him on.

"Let him go," Johnson yelled. "Get in there and stir up Harry!"

Perhaps the Apache couldn't hear, careening on a few feet then jumping clear to fire again. This time Harry's helper spun half around and dropped like a poleaxed steer. In a crouch now Jaime started for the rocks.

Harry in plain panic jumped to his feet and got off three shots. Jaime fired and knocked a leg out from under him. "That's enough," Johnson yelled. "Load them two onto their horses an' turn 'em loose!"

"What about that other one?" This was Amita, coming out of the tunnel looking pale, face stiff, green eyes giving Johnson an uneasy look.

"He got what he asked for. Leave him lay," Johnson said, squinting up at the sky. "Buzzards'll take care of him. This is the real world, kid. It was them or us."

Jaime, working his way up to the ledge, said, "I took

care of Harry. Roped the pair of them onto their ponies and turned all three of them loose.''

''You didn't have to kill Harry!''

''Who's the soft one now?'' Jaime flung back defiantly.

''He was in no shape to come back here again—''

''Crippled up like he was, he was in prime shape to send some more of them after us!''

''But Jaime—'' the girl cried.

Johnson said harshly, ''Leave it lay. It's done. We got other things to think about. Where are those waterbags?'' He looked at the Apache.

''I'll get my horse and pick them up.''

When he returned about an hour later with the filled waterbags Johnson said grimly, ''You're goin' to find mules and all the other things we'll need. I've filled these saddlebags with high-grade ore and here's a list of what you're to buy. We'll pay five men ten dollars a day—you know the kind I want an' be damn sure you get 'em.''

''You mean I'm going by myself?''

''Someone's got to stay here now to be sure this claim ain't jumped. You'll make better time alone. Get started. You can pick up any grub you need at that store.''

Jaime said, dark eyes hot, ''I'm not your mozo!''

''That's right—you're a partner. Now get goin'.''

FOURTEEN

After Jaime had gone Johnson packed up the rest of the loose ore he'd dug from the rockfall, dumped it into the burlap with the supplies they'd got from the trading post, loaded it on Nugget and told the girl they were moving camp.

"But how will he find us?"

"He won't have to," Johnson said. "We're goin' back to the glen. We kin see him from there an', what's more important, we kin spot anyone else who comes sneakin' around."

They reached the glen with the pool just short of dark. "We'll give him a week," he said brusquely. "If he ain't back by then we'll start for Villalobos."

Her eyes were full of questions but she managed not to voice them after a covert look that rummaged his face. It was the face of a stranger, one she had seldom glimpsed before.

He unloaded the horse feed while she hung the water-bags from a branch of the cottonwoods. He then unpacked the ore and their supplies and turned her horse and Nugget

75

loose to enjoy a roll in the grass before quenching their thirst. Then he put up her tent under the hackberries where it had previously been, and recalled something else that needed doing. "Tomorrow I reckon I'd better go back there and plaster whatever ore is exposed—"

"Plaster with what?" she poked her head from the tent to say.

"Mud. So it'll look more or less like the rest of those walls. Just in case we have to pull out of here."

She stepped out of the tent to study his face through the thickening shadows. "You don't really trust Jaime, do you?"

He took a few moments to turn that over. "Again I'd have to say yes and no. About some things I figure he's on our side, willing and loyal. Just where he might go his own way is what keeps me feelin' edgy about him. We've all got things that stick in our craws . . . things we are born with that don't always show, beliefs and distrusts—"

"Say what you mean."

"Well, fer one thing there's this mine. I can see how it might be a big temptation. He grew up around here . . . must know or have heard a heap of things you don't hear him mentioning." Johnson said after a moment, "I'm not denyin' he's been a real help to you, gettin' you away from Villalobos an' all. But he's still an Apache back of everything else. I don't think he wants me in on this deal."

He could feel those green eyes quartering his face, hunting, probing to get under the surface. "Be fair," she said. "Seems to me what sticks in *your* craw is you don't like the thought of teaming up with an Indian."

Johnson nodded. "Guess you've put your finger right on it. He's got a ingrained distrust of what he'd call 'white eyes.' I misdoubt sooner or later, at some critical moment, this is goin' to come out in what he does."

After leaving their camp it crossed Jaime's mind he might get what they needed at Tubac, a small but once-thriving town that was considerably closer than Nogales. He could also get quite a few things on Johnson's list at

Harry's place, which would now be deserted and free for the taking. Pondering this he turned his horse toward the trading post.

He scouted the place with an Indian's care. The three horses he'd turned loose with the pair of cadavers were now fretfully standing before the verandah, saddles empty as expected. Ignoring them he drew up at the hitch rail and, going inside, gathered up four shovels, four picks, a couple dozen sticks of dynamite, about a hundred dollars' worth of tinned food, fifty pounds of corn meal, twenty pounds of flour, and thirty burlap sacks.

Be a fool, he thought, to leave them here for someone else to make off with. What he needed was some good place to hide them. In a dilapidated shed among the outbuildings he found such a place and in just three trips moved all his plunder to this cache. Getting back on his horse he set out for Tubac by the shortest route.

Ten hours later he came into the town, had a quick look around and, carrying his saddlebags, went into an assayer's office, dropping them with a thump on the counter. "What can I do for you?" the man back of it asked.

"I'd like a written report stating the value of this ore."

"Come back in an hour and you can have it. Pretty good-looking quartz. Where'd it come from?"

"Never mind that. Just get it," Jaime growled, and stood where he could watch as the man got to work. "Runs about twenty-five thousand dollars to the ton," the assayer said, looking up. "What you've got here figures about eight hundred dollars." He wrote out his report, put the samples back into the saddlebags and set both on the counter in front of the Apache. Jaime paid him out of money he'd been given for this purpose.

He went into the bank with the report and saddlebags. When he explained he wanted cash money for the ore he was told there'd be a fee, and nodded. "I suppose you'll be wanting this in hard money," the man said, and again Jaime nodded. "I'll take it in gold coins."

"Seven hundred and fifty dollars," the man said, counting it into a canvas sack.

Jaime picked it up, stepped out and got on his horse

and headed for the livery, where he asked the price of mules. Jaime smiled at the answer. The proprietor scowled. Jaime said, "I'll want twelve stout mules. I'll pay seven hundred and fifty dollars. In gold."

The liverykeeper considered him. "Let's see your gold."

Jaime handed him the canvas sack. The man took a look, tried his teeth on a coin, eyed Jaime again. "I'll give you ten."

Jaime took back his sack and stepped into the saddle. He was turning his horse to ride out of the place when the man said, "Okay—it's a deal."

Jaime passed the sack back. "I'll be picking them up sometime today and I won't take no culls." With a final hard look he rode off up the street.

While he was sampling the free lunch in a saloon he told the barkeep he was in the market for five tough hands. "To work in a mine."

"What mine?"

Jaime flashed his Indian smile.

The apron said with a crusty look, "What are you payin'?"

"Ten bucks a day. Each man."

The fellow studied him some more. "You lookin' for trouble?"

Jaime's smile flashed again. "None we can't handle."

"I'll see what I kin do. Come back in an hour."

"Too hot on the street," Jaime said, and sat down at one of the tables. "I'll wait here."

The barkeep called someone in from the back, took off his apron and slipped out the side door. Before the Apache had hardly cooled off the bartender was back with five men who looked, he thought, more like stage robbers than miners. "Line up at the bar and have one on me," he said, dropping some silver on the mahogany while eyeing the female bullfighter hanging over the back bar mirror.

Well, he'd got his five men and wished Johnson joy of them. A meaner-looking bunch of rascals he'd seldom seen in one place. When they'd finished their drinks he said, "You fellers got horses?"

It appeared they hadn't. "No matter," Jaime told them. "You can ride some of the mules."

"Mules!" said the ugliest one.

"That's right. We're taking a dozen mules to the mine. We'll be taking some barrels out there, too. Where's the general store?" When told, he said to the ugliest jasper, "You got a name?"

"High Pockets."

"All right, High Pockets. Take your friends over to the livery. I'll see you there in ten minutes."

Just as he was about to shove through the swinging doors, one of them called, "What kinda mine is this? An' where's it at?"

"Gold mine." Jaime grinned. "Where it's at you'll see when we get there. In fifteen minutes we'll be on our way."

At the merchantile he bought five barrels and two coils of rope. The men were waiting at the livery when he got there. He looked over the mules brought out for his inspection, and nodded. "I'll want twelve hackamores with reins," he announced, and went back inside with the proprietor to fetch them. With a peculiar look the man remarked, "Pretty rough-lookin' crowd. Think you kin handle 'em?"

"We're payin' them ten dollars a day."

Outside Jaime, back in the saddle, said to his crew, "Case of any trouble, I'll be shooting first and talkin' it over later." He pulled the Winchester out from under his leg. "If there's any of you still around to listen."

Johnson spent a couple days at the mine plastering over with mud all the places in the walls of the adit where ore could be seen. He had no idea how much good this would do but he was playing for time to size up the crew before they found out they were into a bonanza.

After this they just mostly sat around waiting on Jaime.

On the fourth evening Amita asked when they'd got through with supper, "Why do you want to go to Villa-lobos?"

"Tell me about this lawyer, Haddam."

"Papa, just a few days before he was killed, had a terrible quarrel with the firm of attorneys who'd always handled our affairs. I don't know what it was about but Papa was furious—said they'd never get another nickel out of him. The old gentleman who was head of the firm had died a few months before, and this was his son Papa quarreled with. The next day he went into town and hired Haddam."

"Name sounds like some kind of a A-rab. What sort of hombre is he—what's he like?"

"Slick," she said. "Much too willing to go along with all Papa's notions, no matter how outrageous some of them were. I'm only going by things I overheard. Overpolite, always so eager to please around Papa. Around everyone else, even more so after Papa was buried, he would act as if he owned Villalobos. He brought in Grue and that fussy Melindroso, sold some of the assets and kept the accounts. Always toadying to Luis and myself—Luis is my brother, the heir, you know."

"Sounds like the kind who would feather his nest. Expect you'd better bring in an accountant to go over the books. That way if he's been juggling things, you can get rid of him," Johnson said with concern in his voice.

"I'm not sure I want to go back. It's not like it used to be when Papa was alive. Everyone going around with long faces, acting like they were afraid of their shadows. He's had several people flogged for what I'd call petty offenses; some of them have left, run away in the night like Jaime and I did. Grue brought in bloodhounds to track them down." Her face grew pale just thinking about it. "If we hadn't left on horses I believe they'd have caught us."

"Sorry I brought it up," Johnson said, and got up. "Gettin' on for dark. I better take a look around." He picked up his Sharps.

Shadows stretched long across the desert floor although the boulder-strewn slope where they had crossed to the mine was still brightly sunlit. Finding nothing to cause any uneasiness he returned to the glen.

"This smugglers' trail," the girl said, looking upward

where it led past the pool. "Where do you suppose it goes from here?"

"Down the other side of the mountain, I reckon. To the tradin' post maybe." He peered upward a moment. "Let's take a look. Funny I never thought about that."

FIFTEEN

Following the smugglers' trail from their towering butte
to the top of the mountain proved far from the easy jog it
had looked. Clearly defined, though obviously not used in
a considerable while, like a snake's track it led back and
forth between the innumerable boulders in ever-increasing
and steepening loops. What had seemed from the glen a
not-too-arduous half-mile climb stretched in the doing to
be well over a mile.

Had they not put it off till so late in the day the view
would plainly have been magnificent with such a vast
sweep of country spread out below. In this fading light it
seemed flat and almost featureless, the whole backside of
the mountain deep in shadow. Yet off in the distance on
the desert floor, looking a mere huddle of whitewashed
blocks, they managed to pick out Harry's trading post.

"Like standing on the rim of the Grand Canyon," Johnson said, the upper half of his body still in sunlight, the
girl's sorrel hair streaming out in the wind. He said, "Be
dark mighty quick. We better head back."

"Do you suppose," Amita said like she was short of breath, "those smugglers were Mexicans?"

"Maybe. Maybe gringos. Prob'ly some of both. Must have had a good two-way business to risk going over this mountain in the dark. To have crossed it in daylight they'd have felt too conspicuous."

"Do you think they were trading with Harry?"

"Don't imagine Harry was around at that time though the store might have been."

Next morning they had company.

Johnson, up bright and early as was generally his habit, got both animals a ration of oats and stepped out on the ledge to scrutinize the slopes and tawny desert below. Straightaway his searching glance found unwanted movement. A lone horseman leisurely approaching the base of the mountain and plainly bound for the smugglers' trail. There was a flash of metal from the rider's vest.

"Better get up," he called to Amita. "We're about to get visited."

He wished he had a glass.

The girl came out of her tent, dressed and bright eyed, sorrel hair put up and held in place by her high-backed Spanish comb. Knowing it would take the man the best part of an hour to get up here, Johnson put on the coffeepot and fried up some cornmeal griddlecakes. They were under the cottonwoods, tin cups in hand, when the sheriff rode into their camp.

"Morning," he hailed. "I'm Johnny Amber, the law around here. I've rode over on a complaint. Couple of fellers smashed up—claim you shot 'em."

"Get down an' have some java, Sheriff."

"Don't mind if I do." Taking the cup Johnson handed him. "About this complaint. Let's hear your side of it. Did you shoot them?"

"I certainly shot *at* them. Came sneakin' around in the dark of the moon. They were warned off an' paid no attention. When they got near enough I let 'em have a piece of my mind."

"Kind of harsh treatment."

"This wasn't the first time we'd seen that pair of rascals. This mountain's private property, legally bought and registered by Miss Pintado's Uncle Eusibio."

"Got tax receipts, has he?"

"Can't say, but I'd imagine so. He bought this land forty years ago. I reckon you can check if you want to go to the bother."

Amita said, "Uncle Eusibio not only had title to this mountain but two miles all around it. He was killed here by Indians."

"And you," the sheriff said, eyeing Johnson, "pretty near killed that pair of ranch hands. One of them fellers won't walk again—"

"An' the other?"

"He'll be on crutches for the rest of his life!"

"Glad to hear it," Johnson said. "Two less claim jumpers we'll have to watch out for." Johnson's eyes looked frosty. "I could've killed those buggers—had a mind to."

The sheriff said gruffly, "We got law in this county. No call for you to shoot them."

"Matter of opinion. If I hadn't smashed up them two we'd be nothin' right now but a pile of picked-clean bones an' that pair would be settin' on top of this mine."

"Where is this mine?"

"You got a warrant? Because if you haven't you're not goin' to set foot in it."

"You're talkin' to the law!"

"Anyone," Johnson said, "can pin on a badge an' call himself the law."

"You tryin' to antagonize me?" said the sheriff, face darkening.

"Nope—just statin' the facts. We've found the parts of four skeletons on this property and sure ain't hankerin' to be the fifth and sixth."

And Amita said, producing it from the pocket of her riding skirt, "This is my uncle's watch which we found in the mine beside his bashed-in skull!"

She held it out. The sheriff turned it over a few times and passed it back, looking from one to the other. "For your information," he said, hard eyes probing, "this property is down in the books as belonging to something or someone called Villalobos—you know anything about that?"

"Certainly," Amita said. "The Hacienda Villalobos takes in almost a third of Sonora. It belongs to my brother, Luis Eladio Pintado y Morales. Before that, just a few months ago, it belonged to my father, Uncle Eusibio's brother."

The sheriff seemed a bit taken aback. He didn't seem for a moment to know what to say, glancing again from one to the other. "And who are you?" he said to Johnson.

"Just a prospectin' citizen—"

"He's Teluride Johnson," Amita said sharply. "A part- ner in this mine!"

"Partner, is he? An' how did that come about?"

"We didn't know, at Villalobos, where the mine was. Mr. Johnson helped us find it and we gave him a quarter interest in it. And Jaime—"

"Who's he?"

"Another partner."

Johnson said, "He's gone off to get us some mules and a crew. Ought to be back before night, I should think."

"Well, mine or no mine you can't go around shootin' every feller that pops into sight."

"In this country," Johnson came back, "the law says a man has a right to protect his property, that a man's home is his castle; and right now this mountain's our home. So you can pass the word around. Tresspassers will be warned off. If they ignore that warnin' they're goin' to be shot."

"Look—" Amita cried, an arm pointing into the desert, "there comes Jaime now with the crew!"

Both the sheriff and Johnson looked where she pointed. Johnson gave the sheriff a comfortable grin. "Stick around awhile an' you can meet the whole outfit."

"Well, thanks," the officer said, "I'll take a rain check. Got too long a ride ahead of me." Slinging a leg across the saddle he set off down the trail.

SIXTEEN

The watchers on the mountain saw the sheriff come off the smugglers' trail and, swinging into the desert, give the oncoming procession a wide berth, passing well out of rifle range.

Asked Amita: "What did he want to do that for?"

"Expect he recollected that old gringo sayin' about caution and courage." Johnson chuckled. "I count six riders, twelve mules—what do you get? Jaime's made good time and I see he's got the barrels."

"But won't they leak?"

"Not after we've shrunk 'em a bit in the pool. And it looks like he's fetched a extra pair of waterbags," Johnson noted with approval. "Should be up here in half an hour. We'll get them barrels off the mules, start 'em soakin' and send everything else—includin' the crew—straight across to the mine. I'll leave Jaime here to tend the barrels. Once they're tight he kin fill 'em up and I'll send a couple of mules for them—"

"Won't you be staying here?"

"Not likely. Somebody's got to keep an eye on them

buggers. For a while anyway I'll leave Jaime here with you.''

They watched the procession swing into the trail, Jaime in the lead with his Winchester across the pommel. Mostly Johnson seemed to be studying the men. "They look like a bunch of bandits," Amita said, doubtfully.

"Yeah. A hard-lookin' lot. Can't say I much blame that sheriff for stayin' out of reach," Johnson said. "They oughta work out pretty well."

Amita said, uneasily, "I wouldn't trust them out of my sight."

Johnson grinned. "My sentiments exactly." He picked up his Sharps and took a squint through its barrel, then went over to where the waterbags hung and got himself a drink.

Jaime rode into camp at the head of the outfit. "Picked up an extra tent," he said. "Figured it might come in handy at the mine."

Johnson nodded, looking over the men. "My name's Johnson," he said, introducing himself. "You can call me boss. You'll be workin' the Lost Padre mine. Get yourselves a drink an' we'll sashay over there. This glen is off limits; anyone caught slippin' over here'll be shot—just keep that in mind an' we'll get along just like two six-shooters in the same belt. You'll be paid when we're ready to start south with the ore. Meanwhile you'll stay at the mine."

"What the hell is this?" the ugliest one demanded. "Sounds like one of them California corporations!"

"That's High Pockets," Jaime said, grinning.

Johnson said, "You got a pistol, High Pockets?"

"Bet your life I got a pistol."

"Might be you'll need it. Just don't start wavin' it round without I give you the word."

It was plain this talk didn't sit too well with Johnson's ragtag crew. "If you've got any complaints bring 'em right to me and they'll get handled pronto. All you got to worry about is keepin' me happy. Soon's you get the barrels off those mules we'll head for the mine—"

High Pockets snarled, "To hell with you!" and grabbed

for his shooter only to stop with dropped jaw, bugged-out eyes frantically staring down the muzzle of Johnson's leveled pistol.

He didn't like anything about it, and liked even less the bullypuss grin stretched across the boss's mouth. "We'll just call this an exception," Johnson told him, giving the pistol a road agent's spin, "and let you off light. Get them barrels off the mules an' be damn careful how you set them down. Next trouble I have with you is goin' to call for a buryin'." He looked them over with a sneer of contempt. "Anyone else got a complaint they'd like to register?"

High Pockets began getting the barrels off the mules, setting them down with noticeable care, while the rest of the crew stared at Johnson speechless. Jaime said under his breath, "This probably ain't nothing but trouble postponed—"

"No need to wait on my account," Johnson broke in. "My trigger finger ain't had a thing to do since I crippled that pair from the tradin' post."

With Jaime leading the way they set out with the mules across the flank of the mountain, headed for the mine. Johnson fell in behind, whistling "Jalisco." Nugget, as if he'd understood the whole thing, seeming mighty proud of his swashbuckling owner. You could tell by the way he swung his tail and the elegant way he put down his feet. It was like he was trying to tell those mules something.

When they got to the level patch leading into the mine Johnson, calling a halt, said, "One of you take this pair of waterbags and start giving these critters a drink. You, over there, start unloadin' your supplies. I want this level stretched out to three times its present size. You'll have to cut away some of that brush and will prob'ly have to move some of these boulders. High Pockets and you other two grab onto a pick and shovel and start in. Them others'll join you soon's they get through what they're doin'," saying which he beckoned Jaime off to one side. "Expect you'd better go back now—wouldn't want anything to happen to our biggest shareholder, would we?"

Right now the animals were his biggest worry, couldn't afford to have them go wandering off; they'd be needing every one of them when it came time to move the ore. He said to his waterboy, ''When you've finished, herd 'em all into the tunnel and see that they stay there. Soon's we get this the way I want it we'll set up a rope corral out here.''

The man he'd put to unloading the supplies had finished his chore and had everything neatly stacked on a tarp. ''All right. Grab a shovel and help with this clearing. I want this to look like the top of a mesa; we'll be holdin' the mules here and put up that tent for a commissary and we'll have those barrels set up out here too. Here—I'll give you a hand with that boulder,'' he said, and picked up a crowbar, laying his Sharps on the stack of supplies.

It was a test in a way to see if anyone, thinking his attention elsewhere, would reach for it or try piling onto his back; but no one did. When they tired of hard work their reactions might goad them into something like that. Right now he reckoned they were sufficiently cowed to accept his orders. Biding their time, he thought with a grimace.

By five o'clock, with a good-sized level suitable to what he wanted to put on it, he told them to knock off. Delegating one of them to get a fire going he started sorting out his edibles and thinking about supper. ''Any of you galoots manage to cook a decent meal?''

A chunky fellow with an old knife scar running from eyebrow to the point of his chin allowed he had cooked a couple seasons for the JH Connected and reckoned he could handle it. ''Name of Wimpy,'' he said, coming over to the fire.

Johnson said, looking him over, ''All right, Wimpy, we'll give you a try.''

He told one of the others where to set up the tent and put two more to cutting poles from the brush which he set where he wanted them. ''Now take these ropes an' string me a corral.'' And when he reckoned it would do they turned the mules into it.

By this time the cook had the grub about ready. Jaime having thought to fetch eating tools, they each picked up

a pie pan and a tin cup and got in line to have them filled.
Wimpy had done himself proud and in a very short while
they'd eaten everything in sight.

"Wood bein' scarce up here we'll not keep up the fire,"
Johnson told them. "You can bed down out here or in the
tunnel—suit yourselves. You'll rise an' shine at five-thirty.
Jimson, there, will feed an' water the mules while the rest
of us are eatin'. I'll take care of the burro. At six o'clock
you'll get to work in the mine. I'll be in there with you
directin' operations."

He did his sleeping out under the stars with an eye and
both ears cocked for trouble, but although nothing unto-
ward got itself afoot Johnson was not lulled into setting
aside his caution. This was a plenty-tough outfit and, given
half a chance—once they'd discovered the value of this
ore—would not be above trying to take over.

With breakfast finished he herded them through the tunnel and along the adit to the place where a part of the roof
had come down, each of them with a hard hat and lamp
which Jaime had fetched back from Tubac. "Let's see,"
he said, "if we can get through this rubble."

It was not hard digging. The problem was what to do
with what they dug out of there. Johnson's temporary solution was to bag it in some of the thirty burlaps Jaime
had got him. The ore he told them to stack against the left-
hand wall. They found quite a bit more of it than he'd
expected. If they realized its richness they said nothing
about it. With no break for lunch and many a nervous
glance at the overhead they had cleared the rockfall by two
o'clock. Johnson went with High Pockets to have a look
at what lay beyond it, about a quarter mile of additional
passage with quartz gleaming bright in both walls. "A
goddamn bonanza!" the fellow growled with a hard look
at Johnson.

The passage ended in a fault, a black gaping hole that
had effectively terminated further progress. Johnson, edg-
ing a football-sized rock from the right-hand wall, tossed
it into that great open pit; it took a full minute to hit

bottom. He said, "Good place to dump all that crap we dug out and we might's well get at it."

Rejoining the others he gave his instructions. "And don't lose those burlaps," he told them. "You boys keep me happy there'll be a good bonus for all of you."

With the passage thus cleared they tackled the left-hand wall with their picks and by five o'clock had four sacks filled with high-grade. "All right," Johnson said, "let's go eat."

Now Johnson had a new problem facing him. Jaime had fetched thirty sacks and he had four of them filled. At the present rate of progress he'd have the rest of them filled in the next couple days. And without even touching the walls beyond where that ceiling had come down. He guessed he'd better have a talk with his partners.

While the crew was eating he climbed onto his burro and jogged over to the glen.

"How's it working out," Jamie asked. "Had any trouble?"

"Not yet, but we'll have it, now that bunch knows what kind of mine we've got here. We've got thirty sacks, four of 'em filled. I figure two days will have the rest of them loaded. Those mules can't handle more than two filled sacks apiece."

"We can get more sacks at the store," Jaime said, "but I see your point. Once we've dug what they can carry do we keep digging or load up the mules and hit for a smelter."

"That's it in a nutshell." Johnson nodded. "If we decide to take off we'll have to take the crew with us—can't afford to leave 'em here. Time we git back who can say what riffraff may have moved in? You've got to figure at least two out of every three hombres round these parts are potential claim jumpers."

"Couldn't we get the sheriff to take over till we get back?" Amita asked.

Jaime grinned. "With this kind of ore I wouldn't trust my own mother."

"And there's another angle," Johnson pointed out. "Say we head for the smelter with our twenty-four sacks and the crew to help guard 'em. Goin' to be a great temptation to that bunch of roughnecks to take over the lot.''

''Yeah. We got a problem,'' Jaime nodded. ''What do you think, 'Mita?''

''I think the further we go with this the more and bigger the problems become.'' She stared at them uneasily. ''If we could get help from Villalobos . . .''

''Afraid that's out,'' Johnson said. ''We can't let you go back there alone—same applies to Jaime. And I wouldn't have no authority there.'' He rasped a worried fist along his jaw. ''And there's Grue to keep in mind whatever we decide to do.''

''We're in a bind,'' Jaime said, ''whatever way you cut it.''

SEVENTEEN

There was no getting round that.

"Would it keep the crew honest if we gave them a share?" Amita presently asked.

Johnson said, "There ain't nothin' but fear will keep that bunch on our side."

"And that not long enough in the circumstances," Jaime grumbled. "We've got a couple days to paper over some of these pitfalls. Maybe I could find us four or five Apaches to keep those boys in line, but—"

"Wait a minute," Johnson said, turning this over. "If we decide to move out and you could maybe get ten we could leave five of them here to hold on to the mine for us."

"And with the other five with us," Amita chipped in, "maybe we could manage. If the ones left here—"

"Didn't decide to become mine owners," Johnson finished, looking grim. "As Jaime said, we've got two days to make up our minds. Meanwhile I better git back there before that bunch tries to keep me out."

Jaime nodded. "Shall I take Amita with me and see if I can locate a few redskins?"

"We sure don't reckon to leave her here by herself," Johnson grunted. "You got any idea where to look for these Injuns?"

"There's a Papago reservation about a four-hour ride from here. Can't say if they'd be interested—some of the younger ones might. There'll be Apaches and Yaquis around these parts, too—and quite a few Navajos, but not near enough to reach and get back again inside of two days."

"Well," Johnson decided, "see what you can do."

With all these things on his mind and no workable solution in sight Johnson was prepared to deal harshly with the first hint of a rebellion. But first he had to get over there and there was no guarantee he wouldn't lean against a bullet on the way over.

But no one opened fire and he came safely into the camp. High Pockets hailed him and drew him aside. "If you was to raise the ante a mite I think most of these boys could be talked into signin' on for the duration."

"I'll think about it," Johnson said, knowing very well a raise in pay wouldn't change anything. He went off to fetch Nugget a measure of oats; he'd watered the burro before leaving the glen. A day and a night in the pool should make those barrels watertight. He'd send someone after four of them tomorrow. There was no way he could get them over here filled. They would have to be filled from the waterbags. He went over to the cook and got a helping of cold corned beef and a couple of leftover biscuits. There was a half cup of coffee left in the pot and this he used to wash down his supper.

It was now full dark. He hoped Jaime and Amita would give this bunch time to bed down before they took off on their hunt for more help. His position already was precarious enough without them knowing he was here by himself.

After a breakfast of beans and canned sowbelly he left the cook cleaning up and took the other four into the adit where they'd been digging yesterday and watched them get started. With any luck he reckoned Jaime and Amita should be back by now with whatever help they'd been able to hire. Most of the Papagos he'd known were big husky fellows, mostly farmers and cowhands, the oldest Christianized tribe in the country, generally peaceful and easygoing, not given much to violence. It was debatable how much good they would do him. He'd have been better off to have hired Papagos for his crew instead of the footloose scoundrels he'd told Jaime to employ. What he'd wanted was a show of force to discourage other persons who might want to jump their claim. People like Harry.

"I've got to see about those barrels," he said. "I'll be back in about an hour. Just keep on like you're doing. By tomorrow night we should have enough dug out to load up the mules an' start for the smelter," and hoped that would give them enough to think about while he was gone.

Back outside he told the cook to put packsaddles on a couple of the mules, and when they were ready he set off for the glen, mightily hoping Jaime'd fetched him some help.

He found that Jaime had exceeded all expectations. Ten husky Papagos were lounging round the pool in the shade of the cottonwoods. "They're not best armed," the Apache said, taking him aside, "but they've all got some kind of rifles, one of them even has a buffalo gun like yours. They're all young and sober and I've given them to understand they're being hired as guards at ten dollars a day. Which, to them, is practically a fortune." He wiped the sweat off his brow with the back of a hand. "Might be a good idea to make Tomasito a sort of straw boss—he's the one with the concho belt. That way, if you tell him what you want done, he can manage the rest of them."

Johnson nodded. "You done all right, Jaime. Let's hope it works out. We'll have them load four of them barrels and I'll take two of them fellers back with me. Might help to keep that crew in line."

Amita came over then to ask how things were going.

He rubbed his jaw and a sigh was wrenched out of him as his sun-faded eyes went over her in unguarded approval. "I just don't know, Amita. Taken at face value it seems like things could hardly be better. But I'll say this, I'm powerful glad to see them Injuns. Guess you an' Jaime are about the best partners a man ever had."

In the way she stood, lips parted, almost breathless, he sensed something he had not glimpsed in her before. The green eyes clung to his in a wondering stare as she lifted her face in the morning light and appeared about to sway toward him while his pulses raced in an unaccustomed fashion. Back in her gypsy garb again, the gamine look of her, sorrel hair caught up in a ponytail, struck deep into him, demolishing barriers no sensible man could allow to fall.

He took a half step toward her but was jerked back into reality as Jaime brought forward the man in the concho belt. "This here's Tomasito, boss. He's waiting to know what you want him to do."

Johnson put out a hand and the Papago shook it. "I spik English a little. You have mine here—right? Mebbeso trouble with crew? My boys heap strong, take care of things for you."

"It's a deal," Johnson said, releasing his hand from the clamp of that grip. "Get one of your boys to come along with us. We'll go over there now and I'll show you around."

The four barrels were loaded on the two mules and Johnson on Nugget led into the trail that crossed the flank of the mountain. The mules came next with the two Papagos following. When they reached the crew's camp the cook glanced up from his culinary duties, peered again more sharply at the tail-end pair in their cowpuncher jeans and the tall undented ten-gallon hats. "See you got some more help, boss."

"Just a part of our outfit you haven't seen before," Johnson said, getting down off Nugget. "Wimpy here's the cook," he told the dismounted Papagos. "Wimpy, shake hands with Tomasito, who's the boss of our guards, a kind of top screw. I've fetched him along to git the feel of this place.'' He could see by the tightened look on the man's scarred face this was not in the category of welcome news. But he shook the Papago's hand. "Make yourself at home," he said. "Glad to hev you."

"We'll be goin' inside," Johnson told him. "Get these barrels unloaded. Put the mules in the corral and the barrels in the tent. I'll borrow your hat so we kin see where we're goin'."

Applying a match to the lamp, Johnson, beckoning the Indians, strode off down the tunnel and into the adit. When they got to where the crew was at work he found they had filled another five sacks. "High Pockets," he said to the staring crew, "this here's Tomasito. He's in charge of our guards. You'll be seein' him around."

There were some comical looks being exchanged among the crew and he could guess their chagrin at not having rebelled sooner. In the tension building up he said to Tomasito, "These boys are good workers. A bit shy around strangers, but they'll git used to you. In a little while, prob'ly, they'll take to you just like ducks to water." He showed his pitiless grin. "Just kinda memorize their faces so you'll know 'em again happen you find 'em in unexpected places."

In the quiet around him you could have heard every heartbeat. Johnson took it all in stride, saying to Tomasito, "At the end of this adit, just beyond where they're workin', there's one hell of a hole. If you're in here sometime without any lamp better watch your footin'." He looked at the staring crew. "All right, fellers. Time to git back to work."

Outside again Johnson told the Papagos, "Don't let one of them bastards ever git behind you. Them's the hombres I hired you to watch. Soon's they've got enough ore sacked we'll load up the mules and head for the smelter."

"You leave them here?"

"Haven't made up my mind. I'm still thinkin' about it. Leave this feller here and when we git back to the glen you better send a couple more over here to keep him company."

"I go with them," Tomasito said.

''With rifles''—Johnson nodded—''an' both eyes peeled.'' He scrubbed at his chin. ''Fill all the waterbags and take 'em along with this dipper and pour 'em into one of them barrels. Everybody over there has got to have water, 'specially them mules.''

EIGHTEEN

After Tomasito with two other Papagos armed with rifles had got on their ponies and set off for the mine Johnson put another pair on sentry duty on top of the butte with orders to let him know if they spotted any riders making toward the mountain. Or any trouble at the mine.

The remaining two Indians he had no immediate work for so he let them stretch out in the shade from the cottonwoods and while away the time as best they could, making sure their rifles were within easy reach.

"Well," he said to Jaime, "guess we've done all we can for the moment. If nothin' boils over we should be ready to load up an' be on our way day after tomorrow. Do you know of any smelter closer than Charleston?"

Jaime stood awhile in thought. "There's a smelter at Contention and another one at Douglas but I don't know if they're closer. Whichever one we pick the shortest way is across country. There's a road from Ajo—say!" he exclaimed, "that's the nearest to where we're at."

"Ajo?"

"Absolutely. Can't be more than sixty miles. Two days' trip by mule train."

Amita, joining them, said, "Will they handle our ore?"

"Don't see why not," Johnson said. "Have to take our turn at the mill, of course, but they'll have an assayer. They kin give us a receipt and some idea of when we can pick up the bullion. Might even make us an offer for the mine."

"Do we want to sell Eusibio's mine?"

"Save a heap of problems if they'd give us a fair price."

Jaime nodded. "Probably send one of their men over here to make an exploration."

They heard a sudden rattle of rifle fire and one of the Indians shouted down from the butte, pointing toward the mine.

Johnson swore, grabbed up his Sharps and yelled at the two lounging Papagos to fork their ponies. He jumped aboard Nugget without stopping for a saddle and headed for the other damp, both Indians right at his heels.

There were no more shots. When they clattered into the camp it seemed as though everything was well in hand. One dead miner lay in front of the tunnel and one of the Papagos had a rag round his arm.

"What the hell set that off?" Johnson demanded of Tomasito.

The Indian said, shrugging, "I dunno. That bunch came out of tunnel shooting."

The only miner in sight was the dead one. "I guess," Wimpy said, "they just don't like Injuns."

"They better get used to 'em," Johnson snapped. "They'll see a heap more Injuns around here than whites. Get that feller buried, then go help 'em get that ore out of the wall. An' you can tell 'em from me they've shot their bonus plumb full of holes!"

When Wimpy stood uncertainly staring back at him, Johnson growled, "They can consider themselves lucky I don't shoot the lot of them. Now when I give an order I expect to see you jump—*andale, pronto!*"

The cook turned pale and reached for a shovel. Johnson beckoned Tomasito. "How bad's that feller hurt?"

"Just a scratch. He be all right. What we do now?"

"Fetch along a couple of your boys. It's time they got a talkin' to," and he strode off down the tunnel without bothering with a light or waiting for help. The Papagos followed him.

It took them about five minutes to reach the scene of operations. There was no work being done. The three survivors of the fracas stood around looking ugly. Two of them reached for their pistols when Johnson came striding into the light.

"Just touch them guns if you crave to end up in the bottom of that hole," Johnson bade them, and spat derisively. "You've knocked that bonus plumb west an' crooked. Any more of these tricks an' you can count on workin' for nothing. Now dig into that wall an' git humpin'!"

High Pockets snarled in a temper and his stare shone black with hate. But with that brash look thinning Johnson's mouth and the rifle-packing Papagos plainly eager to shoot he took up his pick and dug it into the wall; the other pair, no longer anxious for trouble, followed suit.

"I'm leavin' these Injuns with you till quittin' time with orders to shoot the first of you rannies that steps outa line." Johnson growled and, swinging round on his heel, he headed for camp.

The dead man was gone from the entrance and Wimpy, the cook, on the tent's far side was throwing the last shovelful of dirt on the grave. The three Papagos, including the one with the bandaged arm, stood impassively overseeing the job. Sweat streaking his scarred face, Wimpy threw down the shovel. "Fine," Johnson said. "Now dig him up again, drag him into the mine an' throw him down that hole."

One look at Johnson's stare and Wimpy grabbed up his shovel and got hastily to work. The Indians grinned. "See that he does what I told him," Johnson said, and whistling for Nugget took off toward the butte.

When he reached the glen the pair of Indians assigned

to filling the barrels were just making ready to start their third trip with filled waterbags. Amita, standing in the shade with Jaime by the pool, said with eyes searching his face, "Is everything all right?"

"Finer than expected," Johnson answered. "One dead miner and a Papago with a bullet-nicked arm. Rest of those bums are busy diggin' out ore with Injuns standin' over them."

"You still reckon," Jaime said, "we'll be leaving with the mules day after tomorrow?"

"Barrin' unforeseen happenings I don't see why not. With the number of Papagos we've got over there now no one but a fool would be hankerin' to stick his neck out. How you doin' over here?"

"Pretty quiet," Jaime said, "but I'm glad you thought to put those boys on that butte. Don't know why I didn't think of it myself."

"Well, you thought of the Papagos and found us some, too, and it sure has made things easier to deal with. I don't know what we'd have done without 'em. Reckon I better fix us some grub."

"I can fix biscuits," Amita offered.

"Well pitch right in," Johnson said, building up the fire and filling the coffeepot. "I ain't had a man-sized meal in so long I feel like my innards has plumb growed together."

He called up to the watchers, inviting one of them down to get a bit of nourishment and telling the other one they'd save some for him. Evening shadows were beginning to steal across the rocks and on some higher ridge a coyote howled.

After they'd eaten he told the Indian who'd come off the butte to send the other man down and stay up there till morning.

If anyone thought about Grue they were keeping it undercover, as Johnson was himself. He was almost convinced the fellow had given up the chase. No tracker after this amount of time would be able to cling to the trail even with dogs. So he put it away from him, knowing that if the man ever came across this mountain it would have to be through sheer luck or, on their part, the lack.

He stayed up for a while in sporadic conversation with Amita, but finally turned in, too tired to keep his eyes open.

He had no idea what had hauled him from sleep. Somewhere a coyote yapped, the lonesomest sound a man ever heard. Looking up through the branches at a night bright with stars and a lopsided moon sailing high overhead he heard the distant crack-crack-crack of rifles. Throwing off the blanket he leapt to his feet, stamped into his boots and grabbed up his Sharps. Once again he heard rifle fire and reckoned it had to be coming from the direction of the mine.

He lung himself on Nugget and went plunging into the smuggler's trail, bound for the base of the mountain with a Villalobos horse coming hard behind him. "Sounds like a running battle," Jaime yelled.

"It's that goddam crew takin' off," Johnson growled into the wind. "If that's all it was I'd say good riddance, but—look! There they go, straight down the mountain! On our mules an' with some of our sacked ore!"

"Maybe we can head them off! Dodging boulders and weighed down with that ore we ought to reach the desert—There go the Papagos after them!"

Johnson was too intent on the night-blurred shapes of the fleeing crew to waste time or breath in idle speculation. What he wanted was to get those buggers sharp in his sights and you couldn't hit much from the hurricane deck of a careening horse, a fact the Papagos were quick to recognize, all their energies now bent on catching up.

Johnson and Jaime were first off the mountain, both of them hustling to cut off the fugitives. Now on the level Jaime's dun horse forged ahead of the slower burro, spurred on by the bloodcurdling yells of the Apache. Johnson dropped back, too fond of Nugget to push him beyond his capabilities. Also he couldn't see the need with that long-reaching Sharps laying across Nugget's withers.

Another Sharps roared from high on the mountain and

through the moonlaced shadows he saw one of the robbers
pitch sideways off the mule he'd been belaboring. That old
buffalo gun blasted its cargo again through the night but
without any result Johnson could detect.

The pair of fleeing scoundrels still on mules were
scarcely three hundred yards away and about to swing into
the desert when Johnson, already there, although far behind Jaime, pulled up for a probing scrutiny, recognizing
in the foremost rider High Pocket's gaunt forward-leaning
shape almost hugging the mule's lunging shoulders. Sure
got a man's bristles up to see that plumb cultus hombre
about to make off!

Stepping off Nugget and leading his target he squeezed
off a shot. Getting tagged by a slug from a buffalo gun
was pretty near always a terminal experience and High
Pockets left that galloping mule as though he'd been struck
by a lightning bolt.

With the echoes of that shot still banging around that
boulder-strewn slope the sharp crack-crack of the Apache's
Winchester disposed of the last fleeing rider. Johnson, still
standing with his reloaded Sharps, was still quartering the
mountain's flank for the crew's final man when the Papagos rushed into sight on their calico ponies to pull up in
a shower of rock dust and grit. "That's it!" Jaime yelled
but Johnson, not satisfied, hailed Tomasito.

"Where's that dratted cook?" he called.

The Papago headman stuck out an arm toward a younger
companion. "You tell him, boss. He tell me. I tell other
boys."

The pointed-out youth, a moon-faced fellow, told Johnson proudly, "I go Mission school—spik good In-glace."

"What happened to the cook?"

"Oh, him! Scar Face like heap better back there. Him
no leave, boss."

"We better round up them mules," Johnson said, and
the schoolboy put that into his own brand of Papago-Span-
ish and Tomasito sent three others after the mules.

Johnson sent Jaime back to the glen. The schoolboy
asked, "What we do weeth dead hombres?"

"Leave 'em for the buzzards."

"How about hair?"

Johnson, astonished at what he supposed to be a kind of bloodthirstiness, growled, "Papagos ain't in the scalping business."

"True," said the schoolboy. "Papagos civilized. Sometime white eyes like hair for keepsake."

NINETEEN

Back at the mine camp Johnson, having pondered this, said to the Papagos: "Got to have a crew to get out that ore. Right now you're all gettin' ten bucks a day. There's room for four men to dig in that adit. If that many of you are willin' to take a whack at it, those that dig will get fifteen dollars a day instead of ten. Anyone volunteer?"

Every Papago hand shot up staightaway. Johnson grinned.

"That's what I like about you fellers. Not a shirker amongst you, not one man that's afraid of work. But there's only room for four in there. Which four?"

When this was explained by the schoolboy the Papagos held a consultation which resulted in four hefty fellows stepping eagerly forward. Johnson took these back to the adit, showed them what to do and how best to do it, pointed out the pile of burlap sacks. "Put the ore in them," he said, "just like them filled ones you see stacked over there. Okay?"

"Hokay!"

They had all been given lighted carbide lamps attached

to the caps that had been worn by the crew. Leaving them to get at it Johnson went back to the camp to search out Wimpy, whom he found peeling potatoes amid an array of pots and pans.

"Surprised," Johnson said, "you didn't take off with the rest of 'em."

"Well, I'm no fool. Could of told them fellers they'd never git away with it. 'Sides, I like it here."

"All right," Johnson said after studying him a moment, "I'm goin' to raise your pay, but there'll be no cash money till we git this ore to the smelter." Still considering him, he added, "That okay with you?"

"You bet."

Johnson beckoned the schoolboy. "I'm goin' to put you in charge of feedin' and waterin' these mules—understand? When you're not doin' that you'll gather up the waterbags, fill them over at the poolside camp, lug 'em back here 'an fill up these barrels."

The young fellow nodded. "Me savvy. Can do."

Back at the pool he found Jaime eating refried beans and took a panful himself. Amita said that she and the two Indians manning the butte had already eaten, but she'd take a cup of coffee with him, and Jaime observed that things were looking up and prospects seemed favorable.

"Well," Johnson said, "I never been one to count chickens 'fore they're hatched. We got a long way to go before we start pattin' ourselves. Once we string out them mules loaded down with ore we'll make a real nice target for anyone keepin' tabs on this place."

Amita laughed, more like her old self. "With all these Indians to back us up I don't see anything to worry about. Who'd be brash enough to tackle you with them?"

"Three-four fellers packin' buffalo guns out of range for Winchesters could make us look pretty sick in a hurry," Johnson growled. "We ain't outa this yet. Word gets around. Them two cripples from the store will have seen to that."

Jaime, nodding, said through a mouthful of beans, "Told you we should have finished off that pair. Must be a heap of good spots for an ambush between here and Ajo. Don't like to upset you, 'Mita, but we got to face facts.''

"And what if these Papagos turn against us?''

"I doubt that they will,'' Johnson said with a reassuring smile. "As a whole the Papagos are pretty reliable. I ain't never heard of a renegade among 'em. Of course, like Jaime says, between here and Ajo, no tellin' what we'll run into, but I reckon with these boys we kin fight our way out of it.''

He saw Nugget studying her and said, "Nugget, shake hands with the pretty lady.''

Sitting down on his hindquarters the burro held up a hoof. Surprised and with cries of delight Amita shook it. "First time I ever saw that,'' she said. "Why, he's smart as can be.''

Johnson said, "We think so, don't we, Nugget?'' And the burro, getting up, bobbed his head. Johnson gave him half a carrot he dug out of a pocket.

"I remember my mother used to have a little dog,'' Amita said, "and he would growl really fierce anytime a man came near her. She carried him in her reticule and called him Popsy.''

"When I was a boy,'' Jaime said, "I had a dog, too. A great barker. Chief said it kept him awake half the night. He wound up in the pot and all the chief's friends had a piece of him.''

"Ugh!'' Amita said, wrinkling her nose. "What a horrible story.''

"Most stories are kind of horrible,'' Jaime said, "if you're a Indian.''

Johnson stretched out in the shade to see if he'd be lucky enough to catch forty winks. He put his J. B. hat over his face to keep the flies from itching him. "Lot of buzzards sailin' round,'' Jaime said, getting up. "Guess I'll have a look at the far side of this mountain. I never been over there,'' and Amita said, "I'll go with you.''

It was getting along toward the shank of the afternoon when Johnson woke and sat up rubbing the sleep from his eyes. The schoolboy was over at the pool filling the waterbags. "How you doin'?" Johnson said.

"Got three barrels filled. I'm working on the last one."

"Good for you. Pretty hot work, ain't it?"

"My father said, 'A busy man has no time for mischief.' "

"Good thing to keep in mind." Johnson nodded. "Reckon I'll amble over there and see how the boys in that mine are doing." But before he could set out Jaime and Amita came down from the mountaintop. "Seems to be something going on at the trading post," she remarked, and the Apache said, "Pretty hard to make out but there are several somebodies over there and we could see horses in one of the corrals."

This put a frown on Johnson's face but he said, sounding not very interested, "Prob'ly travelers, maybe cowpokes from one of the outlyin' ranches come in for supplies."

"Won't they wonder where Harry is?" Amita asked, looking worried.

"Prob'ly, but I don't reckon it'll bother them. If they're not particular friends of his they'll just pick up what they want an' leave money on the counter."

Jaime said, "Think I ought to meander over there?"

"Only make cause for talk," Johnson said. "Can't see we'd git any good from it."

The Apache scuffed a boot in the dirt. "I feel like we ought to know who's there . . ."

"If it turns out to be Grue it wouldn't help us any if he should catch sight of you," Johnson pointed out.

And Amita said like it made her nervous even to think of such a thing, "Don't go, Jaime. If they don't see anyone perhaps they'll go away."

"If it's goin' to keep you two in a stew I'll ride over there," Johnson said. "Unless it's the sheriff they won't know me from Adam."

Johnson, deeming it shorter, followed the smugglers' trail over the mountain, not that he was in any great rush.

But he had a lot of thinking to sort out and reckoned this was as good a time as any to get that taken care of.

Despite all Jaime's good works and the number of times his notions were proved right—not to mention his sneaking Amita away from Villalobos and the untenable position she was being forced into there—there were times when Johnson lacked considerable of feeling comfortable around him. Nothing you could put a finger on, just a vague unease that wouldn't completely go away. The Apache was, Johnson thought, just a little too ready to terminate people where something less drastic would have done just as well.

These Papagos, too, and despite being Christians, weren't at all backward about putting the white man's weapons to use, yet he wasn't at all uneasy round them. So it didn't seem to Johnson that Jaime being an Indian had brought about whatever it was that stuck in his craw.

And now he'd something else to nag at him. Someone at the trading post. The store, of course, was dependent on strangers, but would folks passing through put their horses in the corral? Not, he thought, without they figured to stay awhile. Finding the place empty in its isolated situation could only look promising to persons up to no good. And once again he was mindful of Brodie Grue, Villalobos's gringo pistoleer.

With this phantom lallygagging round through his notions Johnson didn't like any better than Jaime the thought of somebody settling in over there. He wasn't quite ready to gather up his Papagos and raid the place though he reckoned this was something he might have to fall back on; then it came over him, if eventually why not now? If that bunch at the post—

Johnson delivered himself of a few potent cusswords. The intruders had already become a bunch in his mind, and far as he knew there wasn't anybody there. Be a fool to let Jaime's curiosity stampede him.

Riding on through the thickening darkness he reckoned jumping to conclusions was one of mankind's most pernicious habits.

He'd got near enough now to know Harry's place was

really occupied. Light from more than one lamp was spilling out of the main room's windows. And no horses stood
at the tie rails.

Might of course be the sheriff and a couple of deputies
come over to have a chat with Harry, but Johnson knew
in his bones it wasn't no lawman had put match to those
lamps. The place was too quiet, too wrapped in a feeling
Johnson could not like.

Off at the corrals some horse sent up a welcoming nicker
and, before he could stop him, Nugget skreakily answered. The main door of Harry's place was flung open,
spilling out light around a man's black shape. "Who's
there?" this fellow called, too gruff by half.

Johnson made his decision, said, "The owner, of
course. What the hell's goin' on here?"

"Nothin' as I know of—thought the place was abandoned."

"With the shelves full of stock?" Johnson got off the
burro, stepped onto the verandah, compelling the man to
back out of the doorway.

They could see what each other looked like now. The
man in front of Johnson was not overly tall, he only
seemed that way with his gangling shape; so gaunt, Johnson thought, he'd have had to stand twice to cast a shadow.
In a chin-strapped hat and that holstered pistol tied to his
leg any knowledgeable man could have guessed what his
trade was. Hooked nose, the mouth a tight clamped gash
in the cadaverous face, skin stretched tight and shiny across
the bones of his cheeks.

All this Johnson saw in that first swift glance, likewise
the pair so still behind him. The gaunt man said, "You
make it a habit to go off leavin' the place wide open?"

"We don't lock doors in this country," Johnson said,
stepping sideways to put a blank wall back of him. "If
you've any legitimate business here state it."

The fellow's staring eyes were yellow as an owl's and
held the same vacuity. "Sociable as a hound to a stray
pup, ain't you?"

"When a man finds stray pups on his place an' helpin'

themselves to whatever they fancy, he's got a right to ask questions. My name's Harry—what's yours?''

The man cleared his throat, appeared to check the rush of temper. Something unreadable was at the edges of his stare. ''Name's Grue. We're huntin' a couple of fugitives—one of them's a gitana.''

''Gypsy?'' Johnson seemed to be searching his mind. ''Yeah. Gypsy girl with a Injun stopped here for supplies—let's see, must of been all of ten days ago. Rode a couple horses with some foreign brand—bunch of squiggles,'' Johnson said.

''Them's the ones. Which way'd they go?''

''Got the idea they was headed fer Tucson. Seemed to have plenty of cash. Rob a bank, did they?''

''Somethin' like that.''

''Well, now you know. I'll have a look at what you've picked up an' when it's paid for you kin be on your way.''

Grue began to look ugly. ''We'll leave when we're a mind to. As for what we've picked up it's all there on the counter.''

Johnson grinned, not bothering to look. ''Guess you figure three to one is pretty good odds. Better rethink it, Grue, an' tote up what you've already latched onto. Your bill,'' he said, ''comes to eighty-five dollars an' forty-three cents.''

''Wonder if you're brash as you sound,'' Grue said.

''Put your paw near that shooter an' you'll know for sure.''

TWENTY

"You act like you're dealin' with some kind of crook."

"Right first crack outa the box," Johnson said. "Far as I'm concerned you've got all the earmarks. Put your money on the counter or reach for that hog-leg."

Plainly Grue wasn't used to having such talk thrown at him; it confused him, seemed to put a cramp in his gun hand. Turned cautious he said, "Brusco, put the money on the counter."

The Mexican, hauling up his jaw, broke out of his trance. Counting out the currency from a roll in his pocket he added two quarters and placed it on the counter.

"Now," Johnson said, "pick up your belongin's an' make tracks. You come round here again I'll shoot first an' talk later."

Gone still, the three of them stood hamstrung by doubt. Grue's shape seemed to swell and grow. Johnson's face was like something hacked out of stone. Grue with a nasty laugh headed for the door. The other pair, Mexican and Yaqui, picked up their purchases and nervously followed. Johnson, grabbing up a shotgun from behind the counter, stepped out on the verandah where he watched them lead their horses from the corral, throw on their saddles, tighten the trunk straps and mount up. He got a long hard look from Grue, and then they were gone in a cloud of dust.

Johnson wiped the sweat off his forehead and went back inside. Taking the money off the counter he dropped it in the cash drawer which, of course, had been emptied.

He could feel cold sweat standing out on his back. This was reaction from a bluff that had worked, for he was no more a gunslinger than Jamie. And he could feel deep inside he wasn't done with Grue yet. He'd bought a little time, but that was all he could say for it. He picked up a box of shells and took the shotgun with him when he headed for the mountain.

Amita was in her tent, presumably asleep, but the Apache was still up when Johnson rode down into the glen from the top of the mountain. "Well, what did you find out?" Jaime asked, standing up with the Winchester in the crook of his arm. "They still there?"

Johnson shook his head. "Nobody there now," he said, loud enough to be heard in the tent if the girl was awake and listening. He took the saddle off Nugget and turned him loose to roll and lip at the water. Beckoning Jaime he moved to the far end of the pool.

"Grue an' two others, one he called Brusco and the other a Yaqui. Makin' themselves right at home like you figured. Wanted to know if I'd seen a pair of fugitives, a gypsy girl with an Injun."

A lot of folks think Indians all have poker faces, but Johnson didn't have to look twice to realize the concern on Jaime's. The Apache looked worried. "What did you tell them?"

"Well, I couldn't be sure they'd lost the sign so I said, 'Sure, about ten days ago.' Let him think I owned the place, told him my name was Harry, charged him for the stuff they'd grabbed up, said I had an idea you two was headed for Tucson."

"Did he swaller it?"

"Prob'ly not. But they headed that way when they left. Told him if I saw them around that place again I'd shoot first and habbla later."

Jaime seemed to have a hard time taking this in. "You sayin' he never tried to throw down on you?"

"Expect he wasn't quite sure he could git away with it. I tried to sell him the notion I'd plenty of help within earshot. Anyhow, they're gone; though how far an' fer how long I'm takin' no bets."

"As if we didn't have enough on our plates," Jaime growled, sloshing a glance up the trail. "He'll be back, depend on it."

"Yeah." Johnson nodded. "I'd be considerable disappointed in human nature if he simply rode off and stayed out of our lives."

"You're a cool one," Jaime said, shaking his head. "That misbegotten ape is more to be shunned than a sheddin' rattler!"

"Shouldn't wonder. But for now, leastways, I think he's took off. We'll be movin' out ourselves pretty quick, like as not. How many Papagos ought we leave at the mine?"

Jaime shrugged. Had his mind on other things, Johnson judged. "I figure four should be able to take care of the place. Which leaves six to help us git that ore to Ajo. That sound reasonable to you?"

"I suppose so. Wish I knew what was in that bugger's mind."

"Stewin' about it won't change nothing. I'll have a talk with Tomasito and that schoolboy first thing tomorrow. Tell 'em the possibilities. Right now I aim to catch up on my sleep."

True to his word, first thing the next morning Johnson rode over to the mine camp to powwow with the head Papago. "Soon's your boys have twenty-four filled sacks I'll be pullin' out for the smelter at Ajo," he said, allowing the schoolboy time to translate this. "Expect we ought to have the cook in on what I've got to say," and waved him over. "You kin pass this on to the boys in the mine," he told the youngster.

"Mainly what I've got to say is you're like to have visitors after we've left—one gunslingin' gringo, one frightened Mexican and a Yaqui tracker. Nothin' certain, understand, but it's a fair possibility. *If* they show up they might have some help. Point is," he said, pausing a moment, "don't fool around with them. That gringo, in particular, is plumb mean—you'd be safer steppin' into a nest of sidewinders. Shoot to kill the instant you see him. If you don't," Johnson promised, "you'll never know what hit you."

"Hokay," said Tomasito. "They come here we killum."

"Or anybody else comes snoopin' around."

The head Papago nodded.

"Who are these rannies?" Wimpy wanted to know.

"Crooks an' killers—three times wors'n that bunch you was runnin' with. Keep both eyes peeled."

The schoolboy asked, "What about the mine? You want us to keep workin'?"

"I think you'll be kept busy enough stayin' alive if those fellers show up. What are you called?"

"Roberto Obligato."

Johnson suppressed an urge to smile. "All right, Roberto, you'll be going with the mules to Ajo. Tomasito will stay here to keep things in hand. He can pick out the three he wants to stay with him. There's enough food stuff here to last till we get back."

He described Grue and the two with him, climbed aboard Nugget and went back to the other camp.

Jaime came down from the top of the butte. "How about some breakfast?"

"Good idea," Johnson said. "I'm hungry enough to eat a coyote."

While they were eating another lack occurred to him and he said to Amita, "We'll never git them mules to Ajo on the amount of oats we've got right now—should of thought about that when I was over there. I'll send Wimpy and a couple of the Injuns over to Harry's place directly, before someone else makes away with what's left.''

''But,'' Amita said, ''we don't have the money to—''

''A resourceful man wouldn't let that stop him,'' Johnson said with his bullypuss grin. ''I put enough money in Harry's cash drawer— Anyway, how do you reckon these cow-prodders got to be cattle barons? Not by payin' their way I kin tell you. When you're in Rome you do like the Romans do.''

And off he went to put his plan in operation.

First person he talked to in the other camp was Wimpy. ''See here, Wimpy, we're runnin' short of horse fodder an' we're goin' to need plenty to get them mules to Ajo an' keep them Papago ponies up to snuff. You take a couple of these Injuns and a extra mule with packsaddle and hustle over to that tradin' post an' git us some oats.''

''With what?''

''With both hands, naturally, unless you got a sprained wrist.'' He yelled for Roberto and repeated his instructions. ''Wimpy'll be in charge of this. Just do what he tells you.'' Then he thought of something else. ''How much ore's been sacked up in the tunnel?''

''Eighteen bags last time I was in there.''

''Get after them oats right away,'' he told them, turned Nugget around and went back to the glen.

Thinking for others was getting to be a real chore, he told himself, grimacing, and thought kind of wistful of those good old days when he'd no one but himself and Nugget to worry him. Seemed like the more a man got the more headaches he encountered. Being a mogul, by grab, was no snap!

His expeditionary force came back with two hundred pounds of oats and eleven empty waterbags plus another sack of flour and one of cornmeal. And by late afternoon Roberto, the schoolboy, rode over to tell him the boys in the mine had twenty-four sacks of ore ready to go.

''Good,'' Johnson said. ''Tell Wimpy to give all hands

a bang-up breakfast. We'll be on our way no later than six.''

And sure enough, it was not much past when the long string of ore-laden mules, six Papagos on their eager paint ponies—each man with rifle and filled waterbag—Amita, Jaime and himself, set off down the loops and twists of the smugglers' trail on the sixty-mile trek to the smelter.

TWENTY-ONE

The morning was bright and still crisp with a handful of fleecy clouds high above. Jaime and Roberto led the procession with rifles across their saddlebows and a pair of tall-hatted Papagos on either side of the plodding mules, the sixth Papago riding drag. Johnson and the girl ranged some half mile ahead of the train, separated by perhaps two hundred yards, alert and watchful, to pick the best way.

The mules were held to a walk on Johnson's express orders, his main objective being to get to their destination without loss if this could be accomplished. It considerably chafed him to maintain this pace but in the event they should somehow blunder into an ambush he wanted those mules to be able to run.

When he signaled a halt to give them a breather about three hours after leaving the mine they looked in good shape and, by his reckoning, had come seven or eight miles. But it was warming up now and he thought it expedient to give a short drink to each of the animals.

In heat he knew by experience you had to be careful

about replenishing lost moisture. In the course of his wanderings he had learned the hard way that a man in the desert had a number of rules it did not pay to ignore. And the first of these concerned water. You didn't take a drink every ten or fifteen minutes, and if they were working you never gave animals as much as they wanted.

When they moved on they held to the same formation and the same walking gait. You had to sit on your impatience. You had to keep a sharp lookout for possible trouble. The man who failed to heed these restrictions could soon look to find buzzards sailing over him.

He did not expect trouble from horseback Indians. Most Arizona redskins at this time were peaceable. It was the white renegades that you had to watch out for. You might run into them anyplace and, speaking quite frankly, they were a murderous lot.

They took another brief rest stop at noon, lolling in the shade of a small stand of tamarisks. They took a little more water but did not bother with food. They now had covered, by Johnson's estimate, about seventeen miles.

This was not hard going, the ground they were crossing more or less flat with low hills stretching out on either side, some covered with greasewood and oatclaw, most of them bald. No woods. But as the hours dragged along they went through several stretches of gnarled mesquites and one batch of chaparral which they went carefully around. They saw no indications of water, nor had Johnson expected any.

A lonesome country, much as it had been through uncounted generations.

With thirty miles behind them they camped that evening in a stand of bedraggled cottonwoods along the east bank of a long-dry wash. Johnson built a small fire of dead sticks and broken-up branches, got out his cooking utensils while the mules were being unloaded and was soon preparing a nourishing meal of boiled pinto beans and a good-sized heap of corned beef dug out of cans. While he was busy with this Roberto fed and watered their stock. The Papagos and Jaime swapped tall stories with many a laugh and pounding of thighs.

When all had finished eating there wasn't a trace of cooked food left. Roberto put up the tent for Amita while she helped Johnson clean the pans and black-handled eating tools.

They, most of them, sat around the fire as night settled down, staring into the flames while the windier ones trotted out their best yarns. Johnson posted two men on ponies to patrol the camp, keep an eye on loose stock and be on the lookout for two-legged trouble.

But the night passed comfortably and next morning Johnson treated the hands to saddle blankets—griddle-cakes—and whistle-berries, called frijoles in Spanish.

They got away in good season and by the middle of the day they'd covered another eighteen miles. Since they were hoping to have a store-bought meal in Ajo that night Johnson cooked up a mess of canned spinach and sowbelly and rounded it off with a dessert described by Jaime as "stirred-up dough bogged down with a few raisins and optimistically called 'pudding.'" But nothing was left to be thrown out.

By one o'clock they were again underway, quartering low hills and, wherever practical, cutting around them, always keeping a sharp eye out for trouble. They'd left a plain trail, easily followed by unscrupulous persons looking for loot and, because of this, Johnson had Jaime at the rear of the train with the Sharps across his pommel and a Winchester under his leg. The Apache had argued that this close to Ajo such precautions smacked of the ridiculous. Johnson paid him no heed. "It's when you ain't lookin' fer it trouble hits hardest," he said. "You got a stake in this deal an' you better remember it. Dead men, Jaime, spend damn little gold."

But nobody bothered them and they arrived at the smelter a few minutes after four. With the mules unloaded they were given permission to turn them into one of the corrals and set up their camp alongside of it. Jaime bustled about putting up the tent and Roberto Obligato got busy with his feeding and watering and Johnson said to Amita, "Let's go see what we can find out."

They went into a smaller building where the offices

were, found a door with ASSAYER printed on it and, pushing it open, stepped inside. A baldheaded man in an eyeshade looked up from some papers and got onto his feet when the girl caught his vision. "Yes?"

This fellow, Johnson thought, didn't have no more hair than a Mexican dog. He cleared his throat and declared, "We got twenty-four sacks of ore outside that we've brought here for smelting. This here," he said, moving Amita forward, "is Miss Pintado, owner of the place this stuff come from."

With an admiring glance, "Fisk," the man said, and stuck out his hand. Amita shook it and told Fisk he was looking at Teluride Johnson, a substantial shareholder with the power to negotiate. Then Johnson, fishing a chunk of ore from a pocket, set it down on the desk for Fisk's inspection.

"Hmm . . ." Fisk said. "Looks pretty good."

"Yeah—old mine we're reworkin'."

"That so? Whereabouts? Didn't reckon there was any gold available round these parts."

"This come from southeast of here."

"Near the Mexican border?"

"Pretty near," Johnson said, and the fellow gave Amita another quick look.

"There is some gold in Sonora I understand." He looked some more at Johnson's sample. "When we mill our copper ore we generally get small amounts of gold, silver and a few other metals. I'll assay this for you and if the quality holds up we could probably make you an offer."

"Miss Pintado," Johnson said, "inherited this mine from her uncle who discovered and recorded it forty years ago. She has no intention of selling it. We—"

"Guess I gave you the wrong impression," Fisk said, smiling at Amita. "What I meant to say is this. If the rest of your ore comes up to the quality of this sample I think we'd be agreeable, after milling, to make you an offer for the resultant bullion."

"A cash proposition?"

"Cash or bank draft, whichever you prefer," the man explained, giving the owner another admiring look.

Johnson, too, was rummaging her face. Ignoring Fisk, Amita said with the offhand smile of some great lady conferring a favor, "I want you to use your own judgment in this."

Johnson said, "I expect we kin trust him to make a fair offer. I'll know where to find him if the price doesn't meet your expectations."

The assayer's smile appeared to turn a bit wry as he asked how he was to get in touch with them.

"No need of that. Just give us a receipt and you kin settle for this batch when I show up with the next," Johnson said. "Well, we better be off. Got those six riflepackin' Papagos out there waitin' for their supper," and watched this settle among Fisk's notions.

"If you're short," the assayer offered, "we'd be happy to advance you a couple of hundred." Bending over his desk he scrawled a few words on a slip of paper which he held out with a flourish to the owner of record. "Just step down the hall to the office marked "Treasurer' and our Mr. Bowdene will fix you up."

Two days later with cash money in his pockets and good feelings apparent all around Johnson fetched his outfit back to the mine. No, Tomasito said, there had been no trouble. They'd observed several riders going past through the cactus but none of these had shown any interest in the mountain.

Leaving all but two of the Papagos at the mine with instructions to start digging out more ore Johnson and the others rode across to the glen where he told the remaining pair of Papagos they were to take turns watching from the top of the butte.

Amita and Jaime were plainly delighted with the way things had gone at the smelter. "Wasn't it thoughtful and kind of Mr. Fisk," Amita said, "to arrange for us to have another set of burlaps for our next trip?"

"Well," Johnson admitted, "it was helpful, but the cost

of them will be taken from what they owe us, I expect. You don't get much in this world for nothing.''

"When," Jaime asked, "will we be making the next trip?"

"Soon's we've dug out another twenty-four sackfuls— three-four days, prob'ly. If we ain't interrupted.''

But Jaime and Amita were too pleased with their prospects to consider overlong the possibility of interruptions. So Johnson kept the rest of his notions to himself.

TWENTY-TWO

Four days later, with the mules in good shape, they were ready once again to set out for the smelter. Johnson secretly wished they had more mules, but without means of acquiring more he talked Tomasito into allowing him the use of the ponies belonging to the Papagos left behind.

The Indian horses were not at all partial to being pressed into service as pack animals and for a while they cut up pretty rough while being loaded. Presently, however, all was in order and the outfit from the Padre mine set off with high hearts.

Though you could not guess from looking at his face Johnson's outlook was considerably more sober. He was far from forgetting Grue and could only figure from the gunfighter's failure to reappear that either he was biding his time or had sent to Villalobos for additional help. If the latter was the case Grue must have some way discovered they had found and were working the mine. A very unpleasant notion.

Too, Johnson still had a few lingering doubts about Jaime. It did not seem at all likely the Apache had anything to do with Brodie Grue. Considering past history and what Johnson himself knew of both men it was hard to believe Jaime would side with Grue under any conceivable circumstance. Still, when he and Amita had discovered there were people at the trading post, he'd been—or had seemed to be—unduly anxious to have a closer look at them.

Why?

It was because Johnson couldn't answer this that doubts of Jaime continued to nag at him. Be a pretty serious matter to discover too late there was indeed some working arrangement between these two.

Disgusted by such imaginings he tried to put them out of mind and concentrate on matters which seemed more real and immediate, a confrontation with more of Harry's friends or hirelings, the possibility of being ambushed now that interested persons had been given time to study the route he had taken before.

This, of course, could be varied a bit but hardly enough to make any difference were someone determined to bushwhack them. With all these mules strung out like they were Johnson and party could be considered sitting ducks. They lacked maneuverability and in the nature of things had to pick the easiest going. Their presence, with this many animals, could not be concealed from prying eyes.

So he rode with his uncomfortable thoughts bottled up and wore himself into the fidgets from the constant strain of watching for trouble. Yet the first day of this trek passed without incident; and as evening closed down with its lengthening shadows they made a dry camp in a small motte of cedars, going out of their way to get on higher ground.

That night after supper Johnson doubled his guards. All the animals except Nugget and two horses were hobbled, knowing any attack must be directed at scattering them. Amita soon gave over any attempt to talk with him and retired to her tent, leaving him with his worries irascibly pacing the confines of their camp.

Further disconcerting him, there was no moon and the

stars were cluttered by unwanted clouds and a gusty wind
brought heat up off the desert turning the livestock more
restive than usual.

He was aware of the covert looks Jaime cast him and
when the Apache presently asked what was ailing him
Johnson said harshly, "Look around you, man—the night's
ripe for trouble!"

"Looks calm enough to me. We haven't seen anyone
all day. Probably isn't another person within miles of this
place."

"Wish I could believe that."

"Want me to saddle up and have a look?"

"Yeah—go ahead. But—"

"Keep my eyes peeled." Jaime grinned.

"Fire off that gun if you even *think* you see anything
suspicious."

The Apache picked up his Winchester and rode off down
the slope. This, too, Johnson found suspicious as if,
knowing what was coming, Jaime was taking himself out
of it.

Going over to his blanket Johnson picked up the shotgun
he'd appropriated from Harry's place, a two-barrel affair
which he broke open and loaded from the handful of shells
he'd been carrying in his pocket. He resumed his vigil,
checking his sentries to make sure they were alert. When
he came to Roberto, "Bitch of a night," he grumbled,
and the schoolboy nodded.

"You feel it?"

"I kin smell it in the air. You better wake up the girl."

The Papagos not designated as sentries were stretched
out and snoring among the dark shapes of the trees. Time
dragged. It wasn't yet eleven when Amita came out of her
tent and joined him. "What is it?" she asked. "What's
troubling you?"

"I don't know. Just a murky feelin' I git now an'
again."

"If it's Grue—" she began with a shiver. Then said, "I
don't see how he could know where we are . . ."

"He can follow tracks. A kid could follow the sign
we've left. It ain't just Grue. There's Harry's friends, if

he had any more than that pair I crippled, could have been keepin' tabs on us. That assayer at the smelter—''

''I think you're conjuring phantoms, Johnson.''

''Prob'ly am.'' He scrubbed a hand across his face. ''I hope to Chirst that's all that's eatin' me, but—''

The slam of a rifle burst through his words. Two more opened up from different locations, lashing the night with the crash of their explosions. A horse screamed in terror. All over the camp hobbled mules added to the uproar crowhopping in panicked circles. ''Git down,'' Johnson growled, ''git back of a tree!'' and plunged toward the nearest muzzle flash, firing both barrels, reloading as he ran.

TWENTY-THREE

Everywhere was confusion and turmoil, Papagos trying to
catch panicked mules, riderless horses bolting, and one
rifle tearing the night apart with its racket, continually
firing, endlessly searching for new things to kill. A horse
near Johnson went into the air, dropping back with a jolt
to run snorting from sight. The smell of black powder
swirled through the camp and Jaime's Apache yell burst
against dim-seen struggling shapes and was lost in the
heightened crash-crashing of gunfire. All seemed caught
up in whatever urge drove them, and in the heavier gloom
of the trees where she crouched one single shrill cry came
out of Amita.

That quick, sudden as it had started, with the diminish-
ing sounds still prowling the camp, the whole thing was
over in a fading pound of hard-running hooves.

Johnson, shoving his way through a tangle of shapes,
grabbed the panting girl who fought tooth and nail till he
managed to pin both arms to her sides in a crushing bear
hug, holding her viselike, calming her with talk as you
would a green horse while she got back enough sense to

recognize him. "Is it really you? I'm so glad," she gasped, wriggling out of his grip to stand shaking and battered, eyes locked to his while she pulled great breaths deep into her.

Johnson stepped back, embarrassed and bewildered in the clutch of emotions wholly strange and disconcerting. "You all right?" he growled finally.

"Yes—yes, I think so. Have they gone?"

He said, "I'll go see," but she caught at his arm, holding onto him.

In the first gray light of approaching day they took stock. One dead Papago, three walking wounded, one dead horse, one dead mule, three mules with bullet scrapes and one dead stranger nobody could recall ever seeing before, pretty obviously one of the bushwhackers.

Johnson decided it could have been a lot worse.

Jaime said, "That dead gringo never came from Villa-lobos."

"Never reckoned he did," Johnson nodded. "Different breed of cats. Looks like a townie."

"We going to bury these corpses?"

Johnson took a squint overhead where the buzzards were circling. "Don't expect that'll be necessary. One of them packs'll have to be redistributed and one of them Injuns will have to climb on with somebody else. Let's git at it."

"What about grub?"

"Yeah. All right, I'll stir up somethin', you take care of the rest of it. Make sure Roberto feeds an' waters these critters." He looked around. "We better git away from here soon as may be."

One hour later they shook the dust of that place and set off once again for Ajo and the smelter, which they reached with no further interruptions at close onto five. They turned the horses and mules, after unloading the ore and foodstuffs, into the same corral they had used on the first trip. It being too late then to find anyone at the offices, Jaime put up Amita's tent while Johnson prepared supper.

At eight o'clock next morning he and Amita sought out the assayer.

"Hear you had a little trouble," Fisk said, looking them over.

"Word gits around fast."

Amita said, "This time we've brought you thirty-two sacks."

Fisk's searching stare went over them again. "Sure that ore didn't come from the Dutchman?"

Johnson said coolly, "If it had you wouldn't have seen it. Superstitions are more'n two hundred miles from where this ore was dug out. Four-five smelters nearer them mountains than you are." Johnson's stare began to show a little frost. "You want it or don't you?"

"Oh, we want it, all right." Fisk picked up a pencil. "Thirty-two sacks—"

"Only thirty-one now. We had to repack it after the raid."

"Well, that's close to two ton—call it a ton an' three-quarters."

"Reckon you better weigh it," Johnson said. "We wouldn't wanta cheat you."

Fisk, frowning, sent out to have it weighed. While they were waiting he said, "Haven't milled that other batch yet."

This was a jolt but, thinking it over, Johnson reckoned it was reasonable. Copper got precedence in a copper company's mill. "When do you reckon to git at it?"

"Expect we can run it day after tomorrow." Fisk said, "Get it started anyway. We'll run the whole shebang at the same time."

"What did that other batch weigh?"

"One thousand five hundred pounds. That seem right to you?"

"Close enough," Johnson said, and relapsed into silence. Fisk got back to his paperwork. Amita walked around, examining the ore samples displayed in glass-fronted cases.

Just short of an hour a man came in and handed Fisk a paper. Looking up, the assayer said, "This latest load comes to seventeen hundred and eighty-five pounds, making an over-all total of thirty-two eighty-five," and put all the figures on a scrap of paper which he handed to Amita. "Guess we can advance you another five hundred if you'd like."

"Yes. Thank you," Amita smiled.

"Just take that out to the front office and they'll give you the cash."

"Won't be necessary," Johnson said. "We'll be stayin' round town till you've run the whole works." He glanced at Amita. "Better have him put that on company paper an' sign it."

"Goin' to be a long wait," Johnson said as they headed for town. "Maybe if you and Jaime put up at the hotel time would pass faster. Not much to do in a place like this but if you stay in the plaza you might find it more pleasant."

"I'll stay with the rest of you," she said, searching his face. "Are you trying to get rid of us?"

"Course not—what give you that notion? If you'd like it better Jaime kin stay with the Papagos and you an' me kin stay at the hotel." Johnson colored. "We kin each take a room is what I mean. Give you a chance to look around a bit and eat town fare."

She looked up at him. "Yes. I'd like that."

So they walked along, her arm in his, looking over the sights, Amita in a light blue blouse and divided glove-leather skirt with a flat-crowned chin-strapped Stetson jauntily set on that wealth of sorrel hair, Johnson garbed in the brush-clawed, sun-bleached clothes of a desert rat and a hat that he might have found among the tumble-weeds.

They turned in at the hotel and booked two rooms, Johnson explaining their lack of luggage by telling the clerk they were just off a trip with a mule train and would likely be here for three-four days. "That's okay," the fellow said, "you're not the first that's come here without baggage. This ain't the Ritz but we'll try to make you comfortable." He handed out keys. "The custom here is you pay in advance." So Johnson dug a day's rent from his pocket.

"And the lady?"

"Ugh—sorry," Johnson said, and dug out some more.

"You kin tell," he told Amita as they headed for the eating room, "I ain't done much sleepin' indoors."

Most of the customers were rough-looking men, teamsters and bullwhackers, a few soldiers from the garrison, plus three-four drummers in hard hats and fancy vests. The food was plain but nourishing, the coffee tasting rather better than average. They both took boggy-top pie for a finisher.

"There must be quite a shortage of women in this place," the girl observed, looking round.

"Prob'ly at home with a houseful of kids."

There was a department store midway of the plaza and Amita steered Johnson over to stare in the windows. "Oh," she exclaimed, "look at that hat with all those feathers. Mama wore hats like that when they went to Guadalajara and Chihuahua. Do you suppose we could go inside?"

"Don't see why not," Johnson muttered.

She wanted, of course, to have a look at the dresses. Johnson stood around looking like a steer that had got shoved in with the heifers, and feeling welcome as a rattler in a dog down. When they got back on the street all Amita had acquired was a carved leather purse about the size of a folded-up newspaper.

She hauled him into several other stores too, not to buy anything, just looking, but obviously enjoying this so much Johnson hadn't the heart to gainsay her. They spent most of the afternoon in this fashion and not until she began to feel hungry did they bend their steps toward the hotel once more, Johnson feeling like he'd been hauled through a knothole.

After supper she said, "Let's sit on the verandah."

Johnson hadn't any great urge to make this kind of spectacle of himself but meekly agreed, preempting the most comfortable chair in sight, slouching down on his tailbone, legs stretched out and both boots propped against the railing.

One of the hard-hatted dudes presently came out picking his teeth and dropped into a nearby chair, covertly eyeing Johnson's companion. "Name's Flarrity," he said, "out of Dallas. I'm in whisky—what's your line?"

"Mules," Johnson said, not bothering to look at him.

"That so? My ol' man used to deal in mules. Had some of the finest hard tails you could find in East Texas. Used to bring 'em in from Missouri. You ever been to Missouri, miss?"

Amita shook her head.

"Well, you ain't missed a great deal. Ever been to Texas?"

"Some people," Johnson said, "has got more lip than a muley cow."

The whisky drummer puffed up a mite, his protuberant eyes going over Johnson like he wasn't quite sure where that remark had been directed. "You answerin' for the lady, friend?"

"You might put it that way."

Flarrity dug a cigar from his pocket, one of those little ones that come from a paper box with a tiger on the cover. He started to fire up, looked at Johnson again and dragged out another. "Care to try one of these?"

"The lady don't care to have smoke blowed around her."

"Well, my gosh," the fellow said, getting up in a huff, "it's a free country ain't it?" And when nobody answered he jerked open the screen door and disappeared inside.

"Prob'ly headed for the bar," Johnson said with his lip curled.

"You didn't have to be rude," Amita said, trying hard to keep her lips straight.

"He didn't have to set there runnin' off at the mouth either." Johnson cuffed at a fly. "Didn't even have the gumption to take off his hat."

She did laugh then. "I suppose he thought if you could keep yours on he could too."

Johnson slanched a quick look at her and dragged off his horse-thief hat. "Shucks," he said with a sheepish grin, "you ain't holdin' that ag'in' me are you?"

"No one would ever take you for a lady's man."

"Well . . . no. I should hope not. Where I was raised

they were scarcer than hens' teeth. Fact is, I never had no proper bringin'-up. Just sorta drug up, if you kin understand that.''

"Perhaps I should take your education in hand. Didn't you go to school, either?''

"Yes, ma'am—went as far as the fourth grade. Then, as that drummer would say, I got into cotton.''

"Your parents grew cotton?''

"Well, no, not my parents. But some near neighbors did and they put me to work, draggin' round a long towsack. This was mostly in the fall, so to speak. Winters I chopped wood. Most summers I was a ditch tender. Turnin' valves one way or the other.''

Amita appeared quite engrossed with this history. "And in the spring what did you do?''

"Hunted snakes.''

She stared at him, startled. "Wasn't that dangerous?''

Johnson said with a twinkle, "Only if they bit you.''

TWENTY-FOUR

Tossing and twisting, trying to find some comfort in sleep that night, visions of Grue with his panther's stride and cadaver's face kept jerking him awake until in sheer desperation he stamped into his boots and began pacing the room. What he'd told Amita about sleeping indoors was perfectly true but it was Grue, not four walls, that had hold of him now.

The fellow might not have been on that hill ripping the night apart with his rifle, but in Johnson's mind Grue had been back of that raid sure as sin. If he'd come onto those cripples he'd found out about the mountain; if he'd discovered that much he'd have found the tracks of all those mules and these would have led him or his hirelings straight to their camp. No question about that.

But supposing Grue hadn't been in on that raid? If he'd talked with the ranch hands Johnson had crippled he'd have heard of the mountain and doubtless found it, likely been watching it through one of them brass telescopes the cavalry used to hunt Injuns. Might even have been out there

136

someplace the night of that running fight with those scoundrels Jaime had hired for a crew.

At this point in his thinking Johnson had convinced himself Grue knew all about that mountain. Watching the place he must have known to a man how much help Johnson had to depend on, and if he knew that he'd have known or surely guessed they had found Eusibio's mine and were working it; the tracks of the mule train would have confirmed this, leading him straight to that smelter at Ajo. And, try as he would, Johnson could not fault this line of reasoning.

In narrow-eyed outrage he ground his teeth at not having grasped these notions long since. Now, having done so, it seemed plain as plowed ground that Grue—knowing this much—could even right now be prowling that mountain, probably slaughtering the Papagos left at the mine, grinning as he picked them off one by one.

Johnson could feel the cold sweat coming out on him and suddenly knew in his bones he'd been the worst kind of fool not to have gone straight back to the mountain. And the more he paced the worse things looked. It appeared bitterly evident even if they packed up and left straightaway Grue would have gotten in his licks and taken over the whole shebang.

As a matter of fact, even while Johnson was conjuring these nightmares, Grue himself, having discovered the cheap lodgings in Tubac taken over by the two ranch hands Johnson had crippled, stood inside their room with Brusco and the Yaqui thoroughly enjoying himself after his fashion.

He had both cripples backed into a corner and horribly frightened, the one in a wheelchair, the other on crutches, Melindroso glaring at them over a leveled six-shooter.

"Cat got your tongues?" Grue's tone, silky soft, was threatening as the snarl of a cougar. "If you don't find them in about two shakes I'm like to have 'em out to see what's ailin' them." Giving this time to sink in he said with that sinister grin playing over them, "Let's get down to cases. You found out this jasper was up on that moun-

tain with the girl and the Apache. Some way you got the
notion they had a good thing up there which you figured
just about had to be a mine. So one dark night you two
went snoopin' round an' run into a ambush which, though
you managed to get clear, left both of you too stove up to
do anything about it.''

The one on crutches nodded, licking cracked lips.

"So," Grue continued, "what I'm wantin' is where they
hole up at. You must've conned 'em with a glass before
you ever went near there. I've had a look myself—you
needn't tell me where the mine is or how many Injuns
they've got up there helpin' them. All I want outa you is
the hideout for that girl an' how to get into it.''

The man on crutches said, "What's she to you?''

"None of your goddam business!" Grue fixed his cat's
stare on the man in the wheelchair. "I know they've got
Injun lookouts up there an' I know they've got a camp
somewhere back of that butte an' that there's damn little
chance of my getting up there by the way I've watched
'em use themselves. There's got to be another way into
that camp. Where is it?''

When he got no answer he tossed Melindroso a short-
handled cleaver and with his other hand pointed to the
cripple in the wheelchair. "Lop off a foot—that oughta
loosen their tongues!''

The horrified face of the man in the wheelchair had
gone white as bone. "I'll tell you!" he gasped in a
whispery voice. "There's a trail goes up the backside
of that mountain, goes over the rim an' right down to
that butte . . .''

"An' nobody watchin'?''

"That's right. Joe here's been over there two-three
times. Never saw no watcher.''

With a malevolent sneer Grue told Melindroso, "Lop
off that foot an' let's hear him holler.''

Knowing what he reckoned he knew, it was an awful
strain on Johnson's constitution to fritter away the two
additional days they were forced to wait on the smelting

of their ore. This was still Pima County away over here and in a town this size there was bound to be a sheriff's deputy or two, and on the day following his night of pacing he looked up their office and went in for a talk. The head deputy was seated with his feet on the desk and put them down on the floor before Johnson had got far into his story.

"Lemme get this straight," he said, all attention. "You claim to have found that old priest's mine folks have been huntin' since about the year one. You're tellin' me you come out here with that old boy's niece and a former slave from Villalobos. That the girl, practically a prisoner on the place, made you an' the Injun partners in this mine. That you figure they were followed up here outa Mexico—that right?"

Johnson nodded. "They were followed, all right, by a gringo gunslinger named Grue who was tryin' to force the girl into a marriage. He had the hacienda's cow boss with him an' a Yaqui tracker. I swapped a few words with 'em at Harry's store an' told 'em to git lost or I'd shoot their socks off—a bluff, of course, and them buggers called it."

"An' you claim they been snoopin' around ever since. You figure they've found out about this mountain an' the mine you say is on it?"

"They knew all about the mine but not its location," Johnson said. "This Grue had a map the padre made and on the night she and Jaime—the Injun—slipped away she got hold of the map. In her hurry she tore it, but got off with the biggest part. We made one trip to the smelter with ore—you kin check with the assayer. What I'm scared of right now is this Grue may have killed off the crew an' taken over the place, lock, stock an' barrel while we been waitin' around to git the ore milled."

"I get the picture. What you're wantin' is for me to go down there an' straighten things out."

"You're the law round here, ain't you?"

"Do I look to you like a one-man army?"

"You kin deputize a posse."

"Yeah. Gettin' together a posse for that kinda stunt ain't

gonna be easy as rollin' off no log. Someone's apt to git killed.''

"I've made the complaint, it's up to you to look into it.''

The deputy said, scowling, "I'll look into it, you bet. But if it's like you claim I got no more chance of gittin' your mine back than—''

"It could be Grue hasn't yet got around to takin' it over. If you parade a posse round the foot of that mountain it might hold him off till we kin git back.''

"Well,'' the man said, disgusted, "I'll see what I can do, but don't count on me gittin' anyone shot up.''

"All I'm askin' is that you go down there. You won't need no directions. Just foller the trail we've made with them mules.'' Johnson eyed the man dubiously. "Tell you what: If Grue's taken over an' you drive him out I think I kin promise there'll be a big reward in it for you.''

This brightened the deputy's outlook considerable. He even managed a halfway smile. "I'll see what I can do. How many fellers did you leave at the mine?''

"Five,'' Johnson said, and went back to the hotel.

He told Amita what he figured and what he'd done about it. He thought she looked worried but she said cool enough, "I think you're making too much of this. I can't believe that raid had anything to do with Grue. I think if he'd been there we'd have had bigger losses and he wouldn't have pulled out the way they did.''

"Well, you could be right,'' Johnson admitted. "I don't put much hope in that deputy. I won't rest easy till we're able to git back there. I'm goin' to see Fisk first thing in the mornin'.''

And that was just what he did, got over there before the office was open and stood around fuming and muttering till somebody came and opened the place up.

"Fisk?'' this fellow said. "He won't be round for another half hour. I can let you in if you want to wait in his office.''

"I'd be obliged,'' Johnson grumbled.

Fisk did a bit better than that. Johnson hadn't been cooling his heels for more than twenty minutes when the assayer came bustling into his office. "Just going to send for you. We finished that run last night. We're paying you twenty thousand six hundred and ninety dollars. If you'll stop by the treasurer's office he'll give you a draft for most of it and the rest in hard cash."

TWENTY-FIVE

Amita could hardly believe their good luck when Johnson told her how much the smelter people had paid them. "They really gave you all that money?"

He slapped his pockets. "Draft fer the bulk of it plus six hundred cash. You want to take charge of it?"

"Keep the cash for expenses." She looked pleased. "Why don't you just take care of all of it?"

"Don't like to put all our eggs in one basket." He passed her the paper. She tucked it down inside the top of her blouse.

"Now," he said, "we better git movin'."

They started for the mountain inside the next hour. With the mules no longer burdened with ore they made much better time and set up a dry camp within twenty miles of the mountain which they could see off yonder palely blue against the sunlit horizon. Time supper was out of the way it was dark with a new moon due to show up before morning.

Johnson paid all the hands their back wages out there in the desert where they'd no chance to be fleeced or spend it on gewgaws and firewater. The Papagos, of course, were all for throwing a big celebration but, through Roberto, he managed to get this postponed. He was not at all convinced there'd be anything to celebrate once they got to the mountain.

The morning was well advanced by the time they could pick out its rock-ribbed slopes. Johnson's roving eye hadn't touched any sign of posse or deputy when the mules, following the schoolboy, single-filed into the loops and twists of the smugglers' trail on the climb to the glen.

No lookout was posted on the top of the butte and no smoke showed against or above the mountain's highest scraped-off level where the mine camp should be. These observations thinned Johnson's mouth and lay heavy on his mind as they got into the higher twists of the trail. He drew the Sharps from under his leg and peered ahead from eyes that were scrinched by the glare and darkening thoughts.

With all the racket they were making getting up this trail Johnson had expected some sign of their presence to be evidenced from the main camp at the mine but none was forthcoming. With Roberto and the mules turning into the bend where the trail swung round the buttle Johnson yelled at Jaime that he was going to the mine camp and bade the Apache follow with the mules soon as he put the tent up.

With no idea what the camp would reveal Johnson looked for the place to be strewn with dead bodies. And the bodies were there, lying in plain sight as Nugget carried him up onto the level.

With his worst fears confirmed and the buffalo gun hanging heavy in his hand Johnson felt the bile come into his throat. While his mind still probed the ramifications of this disaster and half his darting glances were searching the camp for the presence of enemies, the crunch of boot-steps brought his head round sharply to see Wimpy come striding out of the tunnel.

"Glad you're back," the cook said with a glower.

"When'd they hit you?"

"Last night. Just short of full dark. Called up they was

traders with a full load of whisky an' them damn fools let 'em come.''

"An' never a shot fired?''

"That's right. Tried to tell 'em it was a trick, but there ain't much Injuns like better than firewater. I ducked into the mine about half a second before them buggers come into the camp.'' He looked around at the motionless shapes. "They only stayed long enough for that feller Grue to pick up a lamp an' have a look where we'd been diggin'.''

"I'm surprised they left.''

"Well, they'd spotted the mule train. Grue had a glass so they knew you was comin'. Then it got dark so they'd no way of knowing you'd gone into camp—didn't know it myself till after they cleared out.''

"Where's Tomasito?''

"Dead with his throat cut from ear to ear.'' Wimpy kicked at a horse apple. "Only one to put up a fight. Never touched one of 'em.''

"Riddled him, did they?''

"Hadn't no need to. Grue was onto him with that great whackin' knife before old Tom could git his gun up.''

"And the others stood by?''

"They was into that whisky like flies to sorghum.''

Johnson could picture it. He let out a great breath. "Can't think how Grue managed to miss you.''

"He almost didn't—guess he was too taken up with examinin' that ore. You might not of noticed there's a short chunk of rock stickin' out jest below the rim of that hole an' that's where I was, hangin' on fer dear life.''

Johnson blamed himself bitterly for the fate of those Papagos; if he'd come straight back or come on last night this couldn't have happened. Wimpy said, "Sounds like the boys are comin' over with the mules.''

Johnson made shift to pull himself together. "Here— help me move these cadavers back where they won't be so apt to stampede the mules. We're short one now—can't afford to lose the rest of 'em.''

Jaime was the first to come over the hump and spotted the motionless shapes straightaway. Some of the color went out of his face. "Grue's work," he muttered. "That's the best thing he does." His eyes sloshed a sharp look around. "Wonder he didn't wreck this place."

"He was in a real sweat to be gone," Wimpy said. "Spotted your train through a glass before dark; figured you'd be comin' straight on, I guess."

The Apache said, "I told Roberto to hold up till I had a look around. We better dig us a hole and get these fellows buried—"

"Hard as this ground is one hole will have to do," Johnson said, "but at least we can give them a Christian send-off. Their friends will expect it. You and Wimpy git started. I'll go talk to Roberto."

Though he must have expected what the boss had to say, the young Papago showed shock as the story unfolded. No poker face there. He went back through the mules to have some words with the others. When he returned Johnson said, "On account of this heat we'd best get them under ground right away. I'll say a few words."

Roberto nodded. "The men will expect it."

After the funeral, with the mules corraled and Roberto looking after them, Johnson rode across to the camp by the pool. He said when Amita came sober-faced from the tent, "Cook was the only one who escaped."

Her heart went out to him. "You mustn't blame yourself. You warned them more than once—I heard you myself. It was the whisky that did it."

Johnson nodded. "I suppose so. But if we'd come straight back they'd prob'ly be alive now."

"Are you sure Grue has gone?"

He stared at her, startled. "Wimpy said they'd cleared out."

"But how could he know if he was hiding in the mine?"

"You've got somethin' there." He stood a moment thinking, then said with a shrug, "According to Wimpy Grue had spotted us through a glass before we went into camp, must have reckoned we'd be coming right on. Cook said he was in a real sweat to clear out." Johnson added, "Musta been scairt half out of his mind—Wimpy, I mean.

He'd have kept himself hidden till he was sure they'd gone.''

"That seems reasonable," she agreed, looking off toward the mine. "Jaime told me you'd buried them."

Johnson said, hoping to get her mind off it, "What's happened to the girl in the gypsy clothes who came into my camp and woke me up to find myself staring up the muzzle of a gun?"

This evoked a wan smile. "That was a very young girl who was badly frightened." The green eyes searched his face. "I've grown up since then. I'm a woman now."

"And no longer frightened?"

"When I think of that horrible man I'm frightened, but not when I know you're in reach of my voice."

For long moments they stood there regarding each other. Then Johnson wheeled away.

He'd been figuring to take her back to Villalobos, but with four of his crew killed this would have to be put off unless Jaime could recruit some more Papagos. He sent a look toward the mine camp and saw about halfway across the slope Jaime with the schoolboy riding toward him. He got a drink from one of the pair of waterbags hung in the shade of the cottonwoods. Might be better, he thought, if they could hire a few Apaches or Navajos.

He found it hard to think what was their best course now. The loss of those men weighed heavy on his mind. When Roberto and Jaime rode into the camp and had cared for their horses he joined them under the cottonwoods.

"I've sorta had it in mind," he said, "to take 'Mita back to Villalobos and settle with Haddam while he doesn't have Grue and Melindroso to back him up; but that's out now. We're too short of men without we hire a new crew."

"If we could get rid of Grue . . . Do you think, Roberto, we might get a few more of your people?"

"You'd have to tell about those fellows we just buried, try to make them understand," Johnson said, "they might get killed."

"Of course"—Roberto nodded—"I would have to tell them that. But if they're to be left in charge of the mine you ought to have a dozen, then those of us with you now could go along with you.''

''Yeah,'' Johnson growled, ''the mine shouldn't be left without an adequate guard. I thought four could hold it but Grue proved me wrong.''

Jaime said, ''What about setting some kind of trap for Grue?''

Johnson thought awhile, nodded. ''Maybe, if he was convinced I'd pulled out he might try the same stunt again. If Roberto could get some more men and fetch them here after dark, I could take you and 'Mita with the crew we've got now and a pack mule or two and set off around the base of the mountain like we were headed for other parts. If we put on a good show there's at least a fair chance he might figure to move in.''

''But we don't want him movin' in.''

''Sure we do if it gives a chance to cut him down. Once he's sure we've gone we could swing back an' come over the top of the mountain.''

''And have him blocked front and rear,'' Jaime nodded.

''At least,'' Johnson said, ''it's somethin' to think about. You slip out of here tonight, Roberto, and see what you can do about gettin' us some help.''

TWENTY-SIX

Night closed in. The schoolboy left.

Jaime, plainly restless, had gone wandering off. "I wonder what happened to the dogs," Amita said.

"Dogs?" Johnson sounded puzzled.

"You didn't know about them? I suppose Jaime forgot to mention it. You see when Haddam brought in Melindroso as cow boss someone suggested it would be a good thing if they had a few bloodhounds to track down runaways. Grue was all for it and persuaded Haddam to buy three. I was afraid when we left Grue would have them tracking us."

"He'd have known, on horses, you'd try to lose them in water."

"Yes. Jaime explained how we might do that. He felt certain Grue would use them."

Johnson said, "All you could hope for by riding through water would be to throw them off for a bit, gain some time."

"Yes. But once we were out of Mexico Jaime said we could lose them for good if we could get into the Rio

148

Grande without Grue seeing us. We gained enough time that we were able to do this. For a night and two days then we rode the river.''

Johnson nodded. "That was good thinking. Having lost the trail—they must have spent hours searching the banks to find where you come out. Once having lost you the dogs were useless—he prob'ly shot them. Once away from the river, of course, you turned west.''

She sounded surprised. "How could you know that?''

"You were a long way west when you came onto me at that spring.''

After she had gone to her tent Jaime came back and sat with Johnson round the fire awhile but they found little to say. Johnson finally got up, declared he was going to turn in and walked off up the trail a piece where he sat hunched up with his back against a boulder. He saw Jaime move off and start climbing the butte with the notion, presumably, of keeping an eye on the other camp. Their remaining five Papagos had gone over there earlier.

Johnson was too stirred up to sleep. Too many worrisome thoughts prowled his mind. There seemed a good possibility Roberto's mission would fail. And Haddam, back at Villalobos, worried him; having looted the estate to the extent of his daring it was almost a certainty the man planned to vanish. But what nagged Johnson worst was the remembrance of the girl asking if he were sure Grue had left. No one had thought to search the top of the mountain.

He was about to get up and have a look for himself when the crunch of a pebble somewhere in the dappled dark above froze him into his tracks.

He crouched in the deepest black by the boulder, listening, and presently the sound was repeated, much nearer. He heard the unmistakable scuff of a boot and lifting his pistol yelled at Jaime: "It's Grue, I think—up here on the trail!''

In the complexity of undefined shadows high above, the slam of a rifle set the echoes rumbling like a mutter of thunder and, closer, came the bark of a pistol. Johnson fired at the muzzle flash, thought he saw movement and fired again and a whimpering shape slid down off a boulder and lay sprawled in the trail. Stopping only to kick the pistol from the fellow's outstretched hand Johnson advanced toward higher ground.

Despite his caution a bit of shale spurted out from beneath his weight. The slam of the rifle almost instantly smashed a slug against rock not three inches from his face to go tearing off in a banshee wail. Johnson cried out and, pretending to be hit to try and draw the man nearer, fell into a bush, evoking satisfying sound.

For perhaps a full minute there was no sound whatever. The quiet was broken by Amita's voice crying urgently: "Johnson!" from somewhere below. "Johnson—where are you?"

"In hell!" answered Grue, his malevolent laugh trickling down through the dark. But no sound of movement above or below. Just a quiet that was horrid with unspoken thoughts.

Johnson hardly dared breathe, so precariously was he embraced in the clutch of bent branches. Above him the rifleman remained motionless as a cat, waiting, watchful, listening, basking in the security of superior firepower.

In a frantic voice Amita called again and distantly, dimly, sounds could be heard from the direction of the crew's camp. In an agony of tension Johnson's legs began to cramp.

A whisper of sound like cloth brushing rock came out of the night to the left of him someplace. He guessed this might be the Yaqui closing in to make sure Grue's rifle had done its work.

A branch began to sag under Johnson's weight and he flung himself clear of the bush in reaction, almost blinded by the flash of the nearer man's six-shooter driving slugs through the bush, one of them snatching the hat from his head. He fired once and rolled, hearing the man with a groan tumble out of his concealment as Grue's rifle once more began to throw up its racket. The Yaqui screamed, drummed his heels and was still.

And now, cutting through the receding grumble of gunfire, a rush of hoofs sweeping rapidly nearer came bounding up from the trail to the mine. Shale clattered above as Grue quit his covert and Johnson furiously emptied his pistol into that flight with little expectation of scoring a hit.

The riders from the mine came pounding into the pool camp below and Johnson yelled down to them that Grue was trying to escape down the back of the mountain. Then Amita was beside him clinging, half sobbing in what sounded like relief as his arm closed around her and the Papagos swept past them, driving their panting ponies up the trail in hot pursuit.

Johnson dropped his arm as Amita stepped back, the pale blob of her face peering up at him. "They'll not catch him, you'll see. He's a devil, that Grue!"

She'd let go of her fright and sounded more natural now she could reach out and know he was right there with her. "Where's Jaime?" she asked.

"Last I saw he was climbing the butte. You go on down. I want to make sure of Melindroso and that Yaqui."

"I'll stay with you. They mean nothing to me."

The two men were dead. Jaime was, too. They found him shot through the chest at the bottom of the butte where he'd evidently fallen as a result of being hit. "Prob'ly lost his balance," Johnson said in a roughened voice. "Fall broke his neck."

And the elusive Grue was still on the loose. The Papagos coming back down the trail some hours later reported having chased him halfway down the mountain. They had lost him then in a maze of boulders. After the moon had come up they had glimpsed him briefly riding off across the desert.

Johnson managed to view his world more brightly when Roberto returned with twelve fresh men and Wimpy dished up a meal that, according to him, was fit for a king.

The recent skirmish, nevertheless, had accomplished one thing. It had left Grue isolated, all by himself. And, first thing in the morning, Johnson with the six old hands set out to hunt him down while the tracks were fresh.

TWENTY-SEVEN

Meanwhile, with three men posted to keep Amita safe, Wimpy had been left in charge of the other nine new hands with orders to resume full-scale operations in the mine. It seemed imperative to dig out as much of the ore as possible before activating an expedition to Villalobos.

Grue's tracks led the pursuit straight to Harry's old trading post where they found fresh sign that he had helped himself to whatever supplies he was about to run short of, including amunition. He had not lingered, it being the consensus of assembled opinion he had left about two hours ahead of their arrival.

Johnson sent one man back to the mountain with a fresh batch of burlaps and piggin' strings. Then on they went, hot on Grue's tracks.

It became plain the gringo was expecting pursuit and was determined to lose them as quickly as could be, seeking out hard ground and several rough stretches of malpais, doubling back time and again, plowing through chaparral wherever he could find it, riding through broken ground and mingling his tracks with those of wild horses

until, by late afternoon, Johnson said to hell with him;
and now, five hours behind their quarry and with night
coming on, they called it quits and headed for home.

It was full dark when they reached camp and got off
their lathered mounts. "We tried," he told Amita, "but
he had too much of a start. Took up too much time sorting
out his devilish tricks. When we finally quit he was pretty
near five full hours ahead of us. We knew that once dark
fell he'd increase that lead. So here we are right back where
we started."

"What will we do now?"

"Rest up a couple of days while we git things straight-
ened out here, then head for Villalobos—"

"But he'll follow us," she said, frowning.

"I reckon he will. Prob'ly shoot up our camps. But
we'll get there," he said grimly, "and we'll get rid of
Haddam if he's still on tap. And when *he* shows up—if he
does, we'll take care of him."

Johnson thought of putting two shifts in the mine, a day
shift and a night one, but gave up this notion, figuring the
men would be too tired to maintain the sort of vigilance
he wanted. There was always the chance Grue might swing
back to hit them again once he determined where Johnson
was off to. There was really no hurry to getting the ore
out. It could only be stockpiled until his return. The important thing was to make sure their claim was not jumped
and taken over by others before he could get back.

By traveling light he figured they might reach Villalobos
in about five days, spend three or four days straightening
out affairs there, and be on their way back. Toting this up,
the mine would be in charge of the Indians for about three
weeks, give or take a day or two. There was simply no
way to improve on this schedule. No matter how enduring
they were horses had to have rest.

Amita suggested they might buy more horses and ride
them in relay. Good horses around here were not over
plentiful and he hadn't any impelling necessity to search
them out; their present stock would do, he reckoned. Then
Amita suggested that with Grue reduced to impotency why

take that awful trip to Sonora when she'd be just as well satisfied to stay right here. "I'd like to remember Villalobos as it was when I was a child," she said wistfully.

But the gamine look was back in her face and Johnson smiled to himself, allowing he could look through a window as well as most. "No," he told her, "there's your brother to think of. What will he be heir to if Haddam is permitted to gut the place? And if Haddam's cleared out he should be caught up with and forced to give up whatever he's stolen or its worth in hard money."

She gave in with good grace. "I think you just want a look at the place; you want to see if it's as fine as I used to think it was. But if I go back . . . Villalobos's people will expect me to stay. When Haddam is disposed of my father's hacienda will be a ship without a rudder. Who will care for it? My brother Luis is too young to understand such things. I can't think what will become of it . . . unless you'd be willing to serve in his place until he is of age."

Now, Johnson thought, we've got all the wrappings off and can have a quick look at what's in your mind. Aloud he said, "Don't think I'd be up to it and someone will have to run this mine. The padre wisely left it to you, knowing how little a girl child is valued in your country." Johnson's smile was bland with guile.

She stamped her foot, glaring up at him fiercely. "I will not be laughed at!" she cried in a passion. "Nor will I go to Villalobos unless you agree to take over its maintenance!"

Johnson grinned. "We'll see."

But he went on making plans for their departure despite this rebellion, telling himself it was a storm in a teacup. And would soon blow over. The trouble with her was she had been spoiled rotten, brought up as she'd been by a doting father who had more of this world's goods than sense.

He conferred with Roberto, asking who of the new hands was best able to accept a position of authority and act as straw boss during their absence. But Roberto had some thoughts of his own. "I am to go with you?" he asked, seeming dubious. "With Tomasito gone I had thought perhaps . . ."

"I'd put you in charge? Would that suit you better?"

"Oh yes, señor. I should like very much to be in charge of this mine. I am a man of principal, of character. I have no bad habits and would serve you well."

Suppressing an urge to smile, Johnson said after appearing to give this much thought, "Very well, Roberto, I expect you will make a fine stand-in for me while I take the *patrona* to her home. You shall be the boss and I'm goin' to hold you to a firm accountin'."

"Your trust," Roberto assured him, "shall not be regretted."

"So which of these men who'll be goin' with us shall I depend on to explain to the others my orders and intentions?"

"I think Joe Hanna could take care of this."

"Call him over and let's git it settled."

Joe Hanna turned out to be a large moon-faced fellow with the gut of a cattle baron spilling out over the hand-carved belt with its silver buckle embellished with bits of turquoise. He had the muscles of a blacksmith and carried himself with an easy assurance, which impressed Johnson favorably; moreover he spoke in the gringo tongue quite as well as Roberto and grasped straightaway what would be required of him. He tipped his head in a sober nod. "I speak, men jump. You will have no complaint."

Johnson, later explaining these changes to Amita, remarked, "Reckon this oughta work out pretty well."

And Amita said, with a straight look at him, "If you're determined to go to Villalobos I don't imagine I can stop you. But remember what I said. Unless you agree to assume control I shall stay right here."

Johnson showed his teeth in a grin and patted her shoulder as though he were Eusibio. "My, what a tail our pussycat's got! Shucks a'mighty! We'll go along like two peas in the same pod."

With nothing further intervening and no sign of Grue to disrupt his plans they set off two days later on the first leg of their journey. He still wasn't happy about several things but Roberto seemed in control of the hands and with guards posted the place seemed as secure as it was possible to make it. The reason he gave the mine so much of his attention was not so much concern over his own interests as because, so far as he knew and had been given to understand, this mine was the full extent of Amita's inheritance. She had nothing else.

He was glad to discover among the six Papagos scheduled to accompany them an Indian who had worked as a short-order cook in one of the Tucson hash houses. This fellow, called Pothook John, was older than the others and tended to be more than a little gruff but was, Hanna assured him, a real top hand when it came to slinging cow-country grub. And judging by the meal he served up the first night Johnson deemed him a pearl without price.

By midafternoon of the third day of travel they slipped into Mexico far enough west of the nearest town to avoid both customs and the Border Patrol. Johnson, with his aversion to rules and regulations, was not minded to be held up by any such foolishness.

On their first night south of the border they set up a dry camp in a rather weird-looking grove of boojum trees which seemed to be growing upside down. Their next camp, Amita assured him, would be alongside a stream she and Jaime had crossed in their flight from the hacienda.

Once again Pothook John proved his culinary worth with a first-rate meal of refried beans and hot rocks—biscuits—topped off with Arbuckle coffee strong enough to float a wedge.

Amita and Johnson, while the Papago cook was scrubbing up, sat around the fire with the rest of the crew listening to gab in a foreign lingo that, as Amita said, might have been Greek for all they got out of it. Then Johnson told Joe Hanna, "Better double the guards around camp tonight. There's bandidos prowlin' these hills and they might take a stab at gettin' off with our ponies."

The Papago nodded. "Mex'kin hair," he said with a laugh, "make good bridle."

The stars came out and blinked at them sleepily. The girl went to her tent and Johnson stretched out with his blanket between a couple of the crazy-looking trees that didn't have enough leaves to wad a shotgun. He was just in the midst of a satisfying dream when the burro gave him an urgent nudge, then nudged him again almost flopping him over.

Johnson sat up, listening into the night, which seemed unnaturally quiet to him with no bats swooping past and no sound of crickets. No sound of any sort. Throwing off the blanket he caught up his Sharps and came to his feet, following the direction of Nugget's pointed ears and riveted gaze without seeing a thing that seemed worth staring at.

But Nugget's ears stayed cocked so he took a few steps in that direction and saw the vague outlines of a crumpled shape. What it looked like in the moonless gloom was a heap of old clothes someone had thrown down. He approached this warily and was about to prod it with a boot when a gun went off at the far end of the trees. Someone cried out. Johnson started running. A horse drifted past, its bulk dimly sensed against the roundabout dark. And now the whole crew seemed to be on their feet and Joe Hanna's hard yell sailed across the camp—"Watch out for the horses!"—and a rifle began blasting the night like a hammer being banged against tin siding.

Johnson fired at the muzzle flash and a single horse rushed away through the murk going hellity-larrup.

Johnson cursed, staring after the sound. Then Joe Hanna was beside him. "One man," Hanna said. Johnson, nodding, steered him back to where the dark shape lay. Hanna struck a match and holding motionless they peered down at what the flame revealed. "Harry Charles," Hanna said. "One of the men I put on guard."

The man's throat had been cut from ear to ear.

TWENTY-EIGHT

They buried Harry Charles on the ridge above the camp with suitable ceremony while the crew stood round with expressionless faces. "A good man," Johnson said with curt simplicity. "A Papago who'll be missed." They buried his rifle with him.

The man who'd cried out when the first gunshot sounded had a bullet scrape across his chest and this they bound up with Indian remedies.

There were three horses missing and while four of the crew rode off to hunt them the rest of the outfit packed up their gear, fed the remaining ponies and watered them. Amita told Johnson, "That was Grue!"

"I know," Johnson said. "He'll probably try it again. Next time perhaps we'll be lucky enough to nail him."

An hour later the others returned with the truant stock and they set off once more in a direction Amita said would bring them to the home of the Pintados. There wasn't much talking, not even among the Papagos. The girl led the way with Johnson riding alongside. Last man in line was the cook with a pack horse.

This was a much rougher country where presently as they went over or rounded one hill after another their pace was seldom more than a walk. Sites for ambush lurked on every hand; the necessity for being continually alert was sorely abrasive to nerves and temperament until the most trifling irritation became cause for an outburst.

Johnson had the girl riding fourth in the column now. The Sharps was sheathed beneath his leg and he rode with the shotgun across his pommel, bloodshot gaze constantly swiveling from one patch of shadow to the next. There was no way of knowing where they'd come onto Grue and the heat and the uncertainty of ever-present menace kept the whole line so jumpy Johnson expected any moment one of these Indians would shoot another. It was like traveling in a nightmare and the agony of this suspense had become very nearly unbearable when Johnson called a halt to confer with Joe Hanna. Upshot of this was to separate each member of the outfit by at least fifty feet, thus reducing the possibility of an ambush wiping out three or four persons at one fell swoop.

Still, this was a nerve-racking business with time, it seemed, practically anchored to the slow crawl of minutes. By noon they had ridden more than twice as many miles as a bird would have taken to reach the same place. A long open stretch ahead promised some relief to frayed tempers. Johnson gave the animals a quarter-hour rest, then pushed on without water or a longer stop for eating.

They would not be reaching Amita's promised stream this side of tomorrow, which, thought Johnson, would be just as well since, chances were, Grue would have set up an ambush there, having scouted the place while chasing her and Jaime.

The place he chose for a campsite was in a group of tamarisks, sheltered on the north by a forty-foot cliff with the other three sides offering an uncluttered and commanding field of fire. Almost at once he put two men with rifles on the cliff as lookouts. He'd have put the whole camp up there except for the danger of having their animals stampeded into a forty-foot fall.

While Pothook John was preparing their supper Johnson

put up Amita's tent. She declared this unnecessary, said she could get along very nicely without it, but Johnson felt she was putting up with enough indignities without taking the final shred of privacy away from her.

With full dark still hanging in the offing the pair of lookouts he'd placed atop the cliff had a good range of vision in all directions, an advantage they'd lose once night closed down. To offset this as best he was able he stationed a man on foot to each of the three open sides at about ten yards from their sleeping arrangements. "I want them wide awake with their eyes peeled," he told Hanna, "and I want these guards changed every two hours. They're to fire at the first sign of trouble. As you must know by now this feller that's hauntin' us is a sure-enough killer. If you don't kill him first he'll damn sure kill you. See that your boys understand this."

The first five hours passed without alarm. With the blanket tied over his shoulders cloak fashion to afford some protection by blurring his outline, Johnson got up with his shotgun then and took up a station between two of the sentries. Grue, he thought, might skip this camp, but the bugger was too unpredictable to count on this or pin down the direction from which he might approach.

He could still hear cricket sound round and about when a blast from a rifle began piling up echoes from off to the left of him some four hundred yards. The panicked whinnying of horses rose through the racket followed almost at once by a rush of pounding hoofs as the animals broke loose and tore past him in an avalanche of sound, paying no attention to the flap of his blanket.

Muzzle flame blossomed from the cliff top. Hanna's voice rose in anger and was lost in a flurry of shouts and yells as the crew got afoot and went streaking off toward the rifleman's position. But Grue was no longer there and Johnson, trying to outguess him, flung himself aboard Nugget and plunged without care at the higher ground leading onto the clifftop.

He caught one glimpse of a silhouetted horseman firing into the camp but before he could get within range the fellow was gone down the far side in a rattle of receding

oofs. Johnson fired both barrels, bitterly knowing it was
useless. He was nearly unnerved when, back at the camp-
ite, Amita called out to him.

Grue's latest coup had just about finished them.

In the first gray light of approaching day Johnson with
Amita and Joe Hanna prowled around through the trees
oting up the result. Of the seven who'd made camp here
ast evening the two guards from the clifftop lay dead at
ts base. The other pair of Papagos, like the horses, were
,one, no sight of them anywhere.

The three survivors stared at each other, none of them
aring to put into words the extent of this disaster.

Johnson, getting hold of his voice, finally spoke. "I'll
ook up some grub an' we'll be on our way."

Amita said, "On our way . . . *where?*"

"To Villalobos, of course."

"Do you have any idea how far—"

"You kin ride Nugget." Johnson's face was like rock.
"We'll git there."

TWENTY-NINE

They found that hoofing it was no way to get anyplace i
a hurry.

It was slow grueling work with heat waves boiling u
off the sand and each floundering stride sinking thre
inches into it, taking real physical effort to jerk clear an
lift for the next nightmare step. It was like wading throug
a sea of sorghum; even Nugget was showing signs of th
strain when after four hours Johnson called a halt. The
wasn't a dry stitch on them and the girl looked almost
wet as the men.

"Be hell," he gasped, "if we ain't headed right," an
poured Nugget a drink from the waterbag slung across h
shoulder. Then he passed it around, none of them takin
more than three or four swallows.

"I *think* we're going right," Amita said, but with s
little confidence this offered little hope. But having no be
ter guide the three slogged on, Johnson's burning gaz
desperately hunting the distorted horizon in a search fo
trees.

Two hours later on higher ground they found a huddl

of dwarf cedars and made a makeshift camp for whiling away the last hours of daylight. Late in the evening with the sun almost down Johnson cooked up another batch of grub, their plight leaving little scope for chitchat. Hanna, wolfing down his food, asked Amita how far she reckoned they were from their goal.

She said, "I honestly don't know."

"Make a guess," Johnson muttered. "Forty miles? Fifty?"

"It can't be that far. Jaime and I, after leaving Villalobos, spent the first night by a stream flowing north, but we made a big circle and zigzagged around while he tried to lose our tracks. I doubt if there was more than ten or twelve miles as the crow flies between that stream and the hacienda."

"Well, we sure haven't crossed that stream," Johnson growled.

"I don't think we saw these trees."

"Doesn't necessarily prove we're off the track. You were headin' west when you crossed the stream. Could be we need to edge south a bit more but continuing east." He put the saddle on Nugget and helped her up. "Be easier walkin' if we stay with this ridge until it runs out. What do you think, Joe?"

"I never been in this country," said Joe Hanna, "but I feel like you. Just a little more south ought to put us right on it."

It was easier going along this high ridge and a soft wind came up to flutter their clothes and the Indian's head-banded hair. As full dark enveloped them it became truly cool as the desert's heat began to be dissipated by the late-evening breeze. Even Nugget perked up, rolling his lip around, sniffing the air.

One hour later they crossed the stream and swung a little more south. At a little past four, going on five, Amita pulled up Nugget and, leaning forward, pointed. Ahead and to the right, perhaps another couple miles from where they'd stopped on a rise, they saw lights.

"Villalobos," Amita said.

* * *

"Now," Johnson remarked, "we don't want to bull into this blind. If Grue got back here ahead of us they'll be fixin' to give us a pretty warm welcome. If I could of had my druthers it would have been you, Joe, who brought Amita into Villalobos. But with Grue on tap that might have seemed too suspicious. Reckon I'll have to fetch her—"

"If," Amita said, "it's your idea to snoop around why can't I go in by myself?"

"What do you think?" Johnson said to Hanna.

"I think," Joe said, "if they don't want her back she could be in some danger."

"Why wouldn't they want her back? Been the whole point of Grue's operation."

"Yes, but not Haddam's maybe."

And Amita said, "If Grue's not here I don't believe I'd get a very large welcome from that abogado. He was always afraid of my influence with Luis."

Johnson couldn't see much logic in that. Luis wasn't of age. He had no say. Neither had the girl. He said to Hanna, "Let's figure Grue's here. If I don't show up he'd be suspicious enough to start lookin' for me. But if you didn't show up he'd prob'ly think nothin' about it. Give you a chance to look around some, which is what most likely we all should be doin'. But if Grue isn't here we could get more done bein' inside straightaway. Day ain't far off an' Grue ain't like to be. Does that make sense?"

Joe Hanna nodded.

They could not get, in this murky dark, a very satisfactory grasp of the layout here, but Amita had told them the hacienda itself was completely surrounded by a ten-foot wall topped with the broken glass of wine bottles, and only one pair of gates as a precaution against roving bands of bandidos and self-professed liberators. That the gates were kept locked with a bell tower overlooking the entire wall in which guards were stationed night and day with high-powered rifles to shoot anyone bold enough to try climbing over.

Johnson said now, considering this, "Maybe 'Mita's right. There's a sawed-off eucalyptus just outside the gates.

We could hide there till we see what sort of welcome she gits."

With no dissension over this the two men slipped into the deeper blackness under the tree while the girl, still on Nugget, approached the gates and gave a yank on the bell pull, making a considerable racket.

A man with a rifle came out of the tower and stepped up to the gates. The paler blob of his cotton *pantalones* and the glint of cartridges in his crossed-shell belts could be glimpsed through the dark. After a low-voiced exchange he went off out of sight, presently returning with a fat man Johnson guessed to be the lawyer, Haddam. In a wheezy voice this one said, "What do you want?"

"To come in, of course. I've come home, as you see," the girl said impatiently.

"You are not welcome here. Go away," the fat man said and, without further words, shambled off in the direction he'd come from and the guard went back inside the tower.

Moving back out of earshot Johnson said to the others, "A fine kettle of fish!" and turned his glance on Amita. "How else can we get in?"

"If we could get word to Josephina, my maid . . ."

"How many servants have you got in there?"

"I think about twenty." She said, eyeing him dubiously, "I'm afraid this is useless. We should have stayed at the mine."

"Didn't suppose you were the kind to give up that easy." He took a closer look at the gates. These were of wrought iron with mostly vertical rods. "I expect we kin get over these," he said to Joe Hanna. "Want to give me a boost?"

"But the guard!" Amita objected.

Johnson grinned at the Indian. "After I'm out of sight make a commotion that will fetch out that feller."

The gates weren't more than six feet tall and with Hanna's help Johnson was soon over them.

When he passed out of sight around the corner of the tower Hanna made a racket by dragging his rifle butt across several of the rods. The guard came surging out of the guardroom. Johnson grabbed him from the back, thrust an arm under the fellow's chin and gave him a whack behind the ear with his six-shooter.

The man went limp and Johnson went through his pockets, tapped him again for good measure and dropped him. Using the man's keys Johnson swung the gates open. With Hanna and Amita, still aboard Nugget, inside he shut both gates and locked them against the sure feeling Grue had not yet arrived.

"What about your vaqueros?"

"They have their own quarters. About a mile from here," she told them. "And they do not like Haddam, or Grue either."

"Good," Johnson said. "Let's give Haddam a visit."

"If Grue is in the house—"

"We'll cross that bridge when we git to it. Lead the way."

THIRTY

The main door was not locked. Johnson motioned them in, followed Hanna and locked it, pocketing the keys. Keeping his voice down he muttered, "If Grue had been here I don't think the fat man would have turned you away." Then, looking at Hanna, "You tied up that feller at the gate, didn't you?"

"You bet," Hanna grunted. "Stuck him back inside that tower."

It was even darker in here than it had been outside. Amita whispered, "The light we saw came from Haddam's office. It's down this corridor," she said, leading the way. "The servants quarters are across the patio at the far end of the house. Haddam's had several of them flogged—nothing short of a fire will bring them out of their rooms." She put out a hand, stopping them before a closed door with light showing under it.

Johnson, turning the knob, shoved it open.

The fat man looked up from a desk covered with stacks of currency he was transferring to a bag by his knee. His jaw dropped open at sight of two rough-looking intruders with guns in their hands. Johnson grinned. "Go right ahead, Haddam. Put the rest of it in an' git up from that chair."

Light from the lamp that was over the desk revealed the wildness of the fat man's stare; and Amita murmured, "Be careful, Telly. There's a gun under his jacket and he's faster than he looks."

"Nobody's fast with a shattered kneecap. Git against that wall, old man," he told Haddam.

The lawyer's wheezy breath cut through the quiet like the up-and-down sound of a saw going through wood. The room seemed on the brink of an explosion. As so often the case with bullies, however, the man was most dangerous when he had the upper hand.

The desperation fell out of his stare and with a visible shudder he got his feet under him and stumbled over to the wall.

Too meek by half, Johnson thought, narrowly eyeing him. What had the fellow got up his sleeve? To the girl he said, "Scoop the rest of that money into the bag an' fetch it here—and don't walk in front of him."

"I've only to raise my voice—" Haddam wheezed.

"Go right ahead if you want your knee busted."

Knowing the Papago to be on top of this, Johnson, pouching his pistol, picked up the bag and tucked it snugly under his arm. Haddam's hands were jerking; he appeared about to cry when Johnson said, "Now git back at that desk an' write me a complete confession of all your actions at Villalobos, the things you've stolen, the accounts you've juggled an' sign your name to it along with the date."

The man, waddling, collapsed in the chair. Johnson, watching, growled, *"Andale, pronto!"*

The man found a clean sheet of paper, caught up a pen with a shaky hand and the girl in a jumpety voice cried, "Where is my brother?"

Johnson thought for a moment Haddam wouldn't answer. The Papago restively shifted weight and the lawyer said, "In his room, I suppose. Where he usually is."

Amita snatched up a candle, put a match to its wick. "I'll look," she told Johnson, starting for the door.

The smell of the half-burnt cigar in the desk's ashtray was strong. Eyeing the man bent above it Johnson growled, "When I count to three say good-bye to that leg," and, about to follow the girl, he told Hanna, "See that he does what I said he should do. We'll be checking it out and if it doesn't shape up he goes to the Rurales an' we'll let them work on him. One . . . two . . ."

A distant crash clattered through the house. While the girl and Johnson stood transfixed a door slammed someplace. Amita, cupping her candle, ran into the hall. Johnson, half-turned to follow, told Hanna, "Prod him a little," and had just reached the door when Amita screamed.

Trembling in the tug of his fury Johnson burst into the hall.

Stretched long and taut, backed up against a staircase he hadn't seen in the dark, with that skeletal arm locked under her chin and the toes of her boots barely touching the floor, Amita's face in the fluttering candle flame was the color of chalk. Above her and back of the banister Grue's mocking features were twisted with glee.

"Made a mistake about her—should of gone for the kid; but that's fixed now. I've got the both of you right where I want you! Drop the gun," he snarled in his high crackling voice. "Do as I say or I'll break her neck."

With a terrible hate Johnson let go of it.

"Now tell that goddam Papago to stay where he's at."

With the muzzle of Grue's shotgun focused right on him and that tightening elbow hooked under her chin Johnson had no choice. With Grue malevolently chuckling he did as he was told, for he could see Grue's finger curled around the triggers.

And now Grue laughed. "So long, sucker."

Johnson flung the bag at him.

It caught Grue full in the face, both barrels of his weapon vomiting simultaneously in a huge crash of sound as Johnson dropped, scrabbling for the pistol below the gaping hole in the wall where his chest had been half a second before.

Thrown off-balance, tangled in his spurs, Grue let go of the girl, his other arm reaching for a support that wasn't there, and went lurching headfirst down the stairs where Johnson shot him between the eyes.

Straightening in the gray light coming through the windows, Johnson dragged a hand across his face with an all-gone feeling at the pit of his stomach. Heard the pound of Amita's boots flying up the stairs and off down the length of an upper hall. He blew out a breath and tramped back into Haddam's office.

The man was still at the desk, badly shaken, looking ghastly, Joe Hanna lounging against the far wall.

Haddam's frightened eyes rummaged Johnson's face. His mouth worked but no words came out. Johnson picked up the paper, reddened eyes scanning it.

The sound of boots came down from above and Amita, smiling wearily, came into the room. "How's the boy?" Johnson said.

"Banged up a little—he'll be all right now that he's seen the last of it."

Johnson passed her the paper. "Compliments of a crooked lawyer."

She read it and nodded. "He's got most of it there."

Johnson's glance went to Hanna. "That bag's on the stairs someplace—you mind fetchin' it, Joe?"

The Papago went out. Johnson said to Haddam, "If ever I hear of you in these parts again this paper, with charges, goes to the Rurales. Understand?"

Haddam, shaking, bobbed his head. Johnson said: "Git!"

"So you're staying," Amita said, brightening.

"Till we git this place into some kind of order. Then we'll go to the mine, send Roberto down here to run the place. How's that strike you?"

"Can we take my brother with us?"

"I'd expect to," Johnson said, and she flung her arms around him.